Midnight's Edge: The Secrets of Sleepy Meadows

Book 1

David Chappuis

&

Michael Klinger

Published by
Melange Books, LLC
White Bear Lake, MN 55110
www.melange-books.com

Midnight's Edge: The Secrets of Sleepy Meadows
Copyright © 2015 by David Chappuis and Michael Klinger

ISBN: 978-1-68046-157-2

Names, characters, and incidents depicted in this book are products of the author's imagination or are used fictitiously. Any resemblance to actual events, locales, organizations, or persons, living or dead, is entirely coincidental and beyond the intent of the author or the publisher. No part of this book may be reproduced or transmitted in any form or by any means, electronic or mechanical, including photocopying, recording, or by any information storage and retrieval system, without permission in writing from the publisher.
Published in the United States of America.

Cover Art by Becca Barnes

*We would like to thank our family and friends
who have always been supportive of
our creative endeavors.*

Characters

Shelly Hawkins-Wickcliff—A young woman who finds herself in the Wickliff mansion's attic and tortured by Jeremy.

Kasey Menze—A young man with psychic abilities who wants to find out what happened to Shelly.

Ethan Hawkins—A confused young man, brother to Shelly, who has just returned to town.

Jeremy Wickcliff—An evil spirit who wants to return to the mortal realm.

Reed Withers—The young son of the town's sheriff who was involved with Kasey.

Rebecca Wexler-Bowen—A young woman trapped in an abusive marriage and has feelings for Ethan.

Rachel Wickcliff—The deceased sister of Jeremy, who he wants to bring back from the dead.

Gaul—A ghoul and servant to the Wickcliffs.

Carol Hawkins—The mother of Ethan and Shelly, who has many secrets.

Edith Ford—The practical mother of Carol, grandmother to Shelly and Ethan, with a past that links her to the Wickcliffs.

Irma Wickcliff—The matriarch of the infamous Wickcliff family who suffers from dementia, mother to Jeremy and Rachel.

Gracey Menze—Elderly adoptive mother of Kasey, best friend to Hilda, Carol, and Lucy.

Hilda Reyes—An old gypsy woman, once part of a coven to rid Sleepy Meadows of the Wickcliffs.

Jason Beckett—A mysterious young man who has come to town to find his real family.

Lucy Wickcliff—The deceased wife of Jeremy Wickcliff, who had once sought to destroy him.

Pit Bowen – The husband of Rebecca who works for the Wickcliffs.

Chapter 1

It would soon be Midnight's Edge or ME as the witches call it, a time of the night when the veil between the living and dead disappears.

My name's Shelly Hawkins-Wickcliff, and I live in the Wickcliff mansion, which sits on a hill overlooking the small town of Sleepy Meadows where I've lived for all of my 24 years.

I didn't know much about ME, but Jeremy Wickcliff did. He was dead, but that didn't stop him from reaching across the realms into the mortal world. You see, although he was gone, he found a way to get inside my head, to manipulate my thoughts and actions, to make my will his own. I've been hearing his voice cajoling me and taunting me for years and on this night, approaching ME, his plan to return to the mortal realm was about to become a reality. I didn't fully understand how ME would factor into it, but to him it didn't matter. To him, I was a pawn in his sick, twisted game.

On this night, I wandered in a daze through the shadowy hallway of the eerie mansion I inhabited. I had heard Jeremy's voice in my head all day as usual, and as usual, he was just as cruel and heartless as ever. This night had been different; I had grown tired of the game. I was no longer able to fight him, no longer able to block out his voice. He had been with me every moment of every day for as long as I could remember. I was tired of the fight to banish him from my mind. I was losing the last grip on sanity that I had.

I was blinded by tears as I reached the staircase that led to the attic. As Jeremy's voice commanded me to ascend the staircase, I wondered why he had wanted me to go there. As I reached the top of the landing to the attic, I heard him call out to me.

"I know you're in pain, and I know how to make it stop. Just be an obedient girl and do what I tell you."

"I don't understand any of this," I said. "Why are you torturing me? Why can't you just leave me alone?"

He chuckled. "Oh, it's almost unbelievable how naïve you are. Do you think it was a coincidence that your perfect fairy tale life turned into a living nightmare? Oh no. I was responsible for it all, princess. I've used the powers bestowed upon me from the other side to pick your precious life apart piece by piece, taking away everything you loved until you were so broken that you were no longer able to resist my will."

"Why me? Why did you target me?"

He ignored my question as he so often had. "Open the door and go inside."

I grasped the knob of the attic door. Unable to stop myself, I opened it. The air was dusty, thick. I could hardly breathe.

He was right. Once beautiful and full of life, I was now meager and weak. I had lost all control of my body and mind, and it was all thanks to him. He'd made my life miserable. He'd convinced me that I was a burden to all that I loved and that my life was meaningless to the point where I started to believe him.

I put my head down recalling the events of the last five years. I thought about everything I had lost because of Jeremy. My husband, my sanity, my life. Even though I tried not to show it, I couldn't control the flood of tears that blinded me. Jeremy knew that my losses had become too much to bear, and he knew he'd beaten me.

"You got what you wanted," I said, scanning the room. "I'm broken. Are you happy now? Why don't you just leave me alone?"

"Destroying your life was just for fun," Jeremy said. "Watching you squirm, cry, and beg were just things I used to amuse myself until Midnight's Edge was upon us, and I was finally able to return to life. That time is upon us, my dear, and soon you'll understand my true motivation. You should be honored, you're an essential part of my plan."

"How? Tell me. Enough with the games. What are you going to do to me?"

"I'm going to help you. I told you I could make your pain stop. The pain of a lonely, empty, meaningless existence."

I felt the warm tears on my cheeks, and my breath grew heavier. "It's that way because of you and only you. If you can make it stop, then do it."

"First there's something you must do for me."

I felt as if he were suffocating me; as if he were holding a pillow against my face as I slept.

"I'm not going to do a thing for a sick bastard like you. Not anymore. The influence you had over me is broken. Do you hear me?"

He cackled. "I don't believe that, and neither do you. I wouldn't waste my last few precious breaths with a lie if I were you."

I put my hand on my chest. "Last breaths? What do you mean?"

"I'm going to live again. You're not."

"You plan to kill me?"

"Not exactly. Think back to what I said to you earlier. Think back to what you said to your daddy dearest when you were in hysterics on the phone with him a while ago. You can remember."

I tried desperately to block out his voice. "No. I won't listen to this anymore."

"You don't have a choice. You never did. I'll never stop tormenting you until I get what I want. You have to know that by now. Try to resist me if you want, but I promise you I won't give you a moment's peace. Now let's get started. Look at what you're holding in your hands."

I glanced down at my hands realizing that I had been clutching a rope. His goal was finally clear to me. Jeremy hadn't planned to kill me. He wanted me to kill myself. "I'm not going to die because of you. You may have taken everything else from me, but I won't give you the satisfaction. I won't take my life. I'll never do it you sick son of a bitch. It doesn't matter what you do to me."

"You have two choices. You either do what I tell you to, or I'll drive you even more insane. You won't even know your name after I'm through with you. What kind of life is that?"

I realized that he was right. I'd known Jeremy was ruthless, but it was clear that his cruelty had no limits. I tried to be strong, to face him head on, but in the face of my death, I'd become just as scared as a little girl.

"I don't want to die, Jeremy," I said, wiping the tears from my face. "Please."

He ignored me and continued to give commands. "Throw the rope over the beam above you."

"No!"

"You can pretend that you aren't afraid, but I know you're weak. You don't have the will to resist me. If you did, I wouldn't be inside your head now. Stop prolonging the inevitable and just do it, damn you."

I clutched onto the rope tighter. "I have a family, a son. I'm not going to leave them."

"They're better off without a pathetic loser like you. You can't even be a mother to your son, always pawning him off on your parents and the help."

"That's not true."

"He's not here with you now, is he?"

Freddy Wickcliff was my five-year-old son. I'd asked my parents if he could stay with them for a little while. I couldn't tell them why. I couldn't tell them that I couldn't care for my son because a psychopath that was inside my head was driving me slowly insane. I hadn't wanted Freddy to see me this way. I thanked God he hadn't.

"That's your fault, not mine," I said. "It's your fault that I'm like this. That I don't have a normal life anymore."

"Is that so? You can't even take responsibility for your problems. You're a sad, pathetic waste. Everyone's sick of always having to tiptoe around you, always covering for you."

I wiped the tears from my cheeks. "Shut up!"

"You'd be doing everyone a favor if you put an end to this. If you truly loved them, you'd take the burden off."

"You can't control me anymore. I won't let you."

"Oh really? Look at what you've done."

I looked around me. Without even realizing it, I'd fashioned a noose from the rope and threw it on the beam above where I stood. I'd also moved a chair underneath and stood on it.

"See?" he said. "You know I'm right. For your sake and for the sake of those you supposedly love, end this now."

I stood there, finally defeated. Long soaked strands of my dark hair drenched with sweat and tears dangled in my face. I had thought that if my life were over, I'd never have to listen to him again. Maybe he was right; maybe my family was better off without me. Maybe I could find peace if I were dead, and so could they, no longer having to deal with my problems.

With no more will to fight, I slipped my head into the noose and took a deep breath.

"Good girl," were the final words I heard as I stepped off the chair.

Within a few moments, everything went dark.

The darkness only lasted for an instant. I opened my eyes and couldn't breathe. The noose around my neck was suffocating me. I clutched at the rope with both hands, frantically trying to break free, fumbling with it fruitlessly.

I realized that I only had a few precious moments before it would be too late, and Jeremy would get what he wanted. I couldn't let that happen. I thought of my parents, brother, son, and everything I would leave behind if I were to go through with this. I knew I had to keep fighting for them even more than I did for myself.

With one last gasp of air and one last ounce of strength, I undid the knot and slid my head out of the noose.

I fell to the floor without a thump, which I thought odd. I gasped for air and clutched my throat. It took me a moment to get my breath back, but once I did, I felt a sense of relief that I'd never before felt. I was alive and so immensely grateful.

I got up quickly, surprised that I wasn't hurt in the fall, thankful I hadn't succeeded. More tears formed in my eyes. They were tears of joy, relief, and frustration for even considering Jeremy's sick request. I didn't want to waste time thinking about him. Instead, I wanted to focus on my son, whom I had almost left an orphan. He'd already lost his father, and I knew that I couldn't allow him to lose me too.

I glanced around the room, chuckling triumphantly. "It didn't work, Jeremy! Do you hear that? It didn't work."

Jeremy. Why hadn't I heard his voice any longer? He hadn't given me a moment's peace before. I stood there wondering why he wasn't goading me on anymore. Maybe it meant that I'd won. Maybe since my suicide had failed, I'd conquered him.

Maybe it was finally over.

I took in a deep breath, turned around and glanced up at the ceiling. My relief soon turned to horror when I saw that the noose I had fastened

wasn't empty at all.
    There, still hanging from the rafters, was my body.

Chapter 2

The sight of it repulsed me. It hung limp and lifeless; my hair hung in snake-like strands down my face, which had turned blue, almost the same color as the nightgown I'd been wearing.

I covered my mouth with my hands and held a scream back, wondering how this could be. It had to be some mistake.

I quickly touched my face, arms, and legs. I felt my heart in my chest beating fast and could smell the dank, musty odor of the attic that had been closed for so many years. Hundreds of cobwebs surrounded me, covering the rafters and items that had long been forgotten. Crickets chirped in the background.

My senses worked, my heart was beating. I had to be alive. With as much courage as I could muster, I approached my body. I tried to touch it, only to have my hand go through it as if it were a mirage that wasn't there.

I cried out, unable to suppress my emotion as the realization set in that this was all real. My suicide had been successful and my life as I knew it was over. "You made me do this! You sick, twisted bastard!"

I glared at my body, wishing that I'd told my deceased husband, Rory, when he'd been alive that I'd heard Jeremy's voice in my head. Maybe if I had, I could've avoided the disastrous consequences for both of us. I'd feared that he'd think I was crazy. Maybe he would have, but at least we'd both still be alive.

My sadness and grief turned to anger. I clenched my fists and shook them uncontrollably. "I hate you, Jeremy! Wherever you are, I hope you're suffering as much as you've made me suffer."

I stopped suddenly when I heard his voice again.

"Psst. Behind you."

I whipped around seeing nothing but a large painting leaning against the wall. Jeremy's evil, cold laughter filled the air.

I stepped closer to the painting; it was a large portrait of Jeremy. Although he was heartless on the inside, he'd been good looking. He had blond hair and piercing green eyes that seemed to look through me. That's what I was afraid of. I'd asked the Wickcliff manservant, Gaul, to bring it up here months prior, hoping, praying that if the portrait had been out of sight that Jeremy could no longer get to me.

It was useless, and now, even in death, I couldn't get rid of him. "I did what you wanted. You promised you'd leave me alone. Haven't you tortured me enough?"

Jeremy's image moved inside the portrait, making me stumble backward. He gave me a malicious grin. "I'll decide when you've had enough. And as far as that promise goes, I'm afraid it was made to be broken."

"If I'm dead, why aren't you here? Where are all the other people who have crossed over? Why am I alone here?"

"Just because we're dead, doesn't mean we're in the same place. There's more than one realm a person can enter in the afterlife."

"Realm? I'm not going to heaven, you mean? Is it my punishment for my suicide to be trapped here with you? Is this hell?"

"There's a lot more to death than heaven and hell. You have a lot to learn. You are in the spirit realm." He pointed to my body in the noose. "Your body is in the mortal realm where I plan to return. The realms are like an in-between place, not heaven or hell."

"If you're not with me in the spirit realm, where are you?"

"The ghost realm, the one closest to the mortals. That's why I was able to contact you."

"I hope you rot there forever."

His eyes narrowed. "I'll be out of here soon enough at Midnight's Edge. Because of what you've done my plan is coming together quite nicely, and soon I'll be able to go back to the mortal realm and live again."

My insides boiled. "How?"

"That's none of your concern. You served your purpose."

"I should destroy you now while I have the chance, slice this painting to shreds. I should've done it long ago."

I reached for the portrait but was unable to pick it up. My hands passed right through it.

He covered his mouth and snickered. "You're dead. You can't just touch things. The rules have changed. You wouldn't know anything. You're just a stupid twit who threw her life away and is now all alone. At least in death you've enabled me to live again. You're worth more dead than you were alive." He shook his head, amused. "It's no wonder why you were such an easy target. Getting you to do whatever I said was hardly any challenge at all. You took all the fun right out of it."

"You don't have any power over me anymore. Say whatever you'd like. It can't affect me like it used to."

"It doesn't matter. I no longer need you. Your death gave me the strength I'll need to make contact with another mortal, and this time I'll be strong enough to be reborn, invincible and indestructible."

"You keep saying that. My death will allow you to live. Why do you have to keep talking in riddles? Why can't you just give me a straight answer for once? I think you at least owe me an explanation."

"I owe you nothing…but I suppose I can tell you. You can't do anything to stop me now. I found strength in your fear and confidence in your anxiety. I fed off of it and now, because of you, I'll get exactly what I deserve."

"You mean that you're going to burn in hell?"

He sneered. "You're a pathetic bitch. I'm so sick of your snide little comments. You're nothing to me. I don't even know why I'm talking to you."

"Why are you then? Maybe your plan isn't working so well. You're not alive. You're still stuck in that painting."

"My plan will work. I'm just talking to you because I'm bored. I need something to do while I wait for someone to release me."

"And then what?"

"If I'm going to live again, I need someone strong and virile to find my portrait at Midnight's Edge, which is fast approaching. I can get inside their head as I did yours. Only now, I'm strong enough not only to take over their mind but their body too."

"That'll never happen. Nobody ever comes up here."

"You did, thanks to me. Gaul's my servant and he's not like

everyone else. He's the walking dead, and he's closer to my realm then he is to the mortal one. I've been able to communicate with him because of that, and he has his instructions. He'll come up here, find you, and lure some unsuspecting fool here because of it. That's when I'll make my move. Now do you see why you had to die?"

I said nothing, trying not to let him know that he was upsetting me.

"That's right, Shelly. Gaul finding you will be the next step in my rebirth, and I couldn't have accomplished it without you."

I turned my back on him, realizing I'd made a fatal error. I thought about my family and what they'd have to endure finding out that I was dead. I was also concerned about what would happen to them once Jeremy was alive again. If he tortured me and relished in the fact that he stole my life, I doubted that he would leave my family alone.

"Oh, God. What've I done?"

"I'm honored that you think so highly of me, but I'm not God. And I'm afraid that if there were a God, he couldn't help you now."

I turned to him again. His image faded away from the portrait leaving nothing but black canvas. I was left there alone, distraught over what I had done. I couldn't believe that I'd been this stupid.

I turned around and saw a small window, went up to it and looked out. The moon lit up the small town below. Everything looked the same as it had when I was alive.

I desperately had to get out of the attic. Although I didn't know how I would make contact with them, I knew that the only chance I had to warn those I loved that they could be in danger was to get out of the attic.

I went to the door and, as with my body and Jeremy's painting, when I tried to grasp the knob, my hand passed through it. The same thing happened when I tried to put my hand on the window casing to open the window. Realizing for the first time that I was trapped, I began to panic. My breathing intensified, and my heart beat so fast I could feel it. I felt scared and alone.

I wished that my older brother Ethan were here. He'd know what to do. He'd been so comforting the last time that I had talked to him about how overwhelming my life had become. I didn't tell him about Jeremy and what he was doing to me, but just knowing that he cared meant a lot.I was sure that he'd be able to help me somehow.

As I continued to think of Ethan, a picture formed in my mind. It was unclear at first, but the longer I thought of him, and the harder I concentrated, the clearer and sharper the image became. It was like a movie, yet it was happening.

I began to see him driving in his beat up Chevy. It looked as though he was driving through Sleepy Meadows. I didn't even realize he was coming back to town. He'd moved away five years ago after Rory died and hadn't come back.

It looked as if he were headed to the docks. I focused all my energy on him and nothing but him. I continued to concentrate on my brother and soon realized that not only could I see him, but I could also read his thoughts. I could feel his emotions. Jeremy didn't hold all the cards after all.

I didn't understand my new abilities, but if I were able to see Ethan and read his thoughts, maybe I could do the same with the rest of my loved ones. I began to wonder if this were the real reason I'd died. Not so that Jeremy could return to life, but so I could learn about his plans and use my newfound abilities as a spirit to stop him from succeeding.

Chapter 3

Although my spirit body was still trapped in the Wickcliff attic, my mind was free. I began to realize that I could go places in my mind, and right now I wanted the comfort of my older brother, even if he didn't know I was there.

I watched as Ethan entered the town and reached the docks where our father had some fishing boats. Despite the late hour, he wanted to go there first because when we were kids, the water had a calming effect on him, and it still did.

Even though he hadn't yet known about me, he'd known that I was in trouble from the last conversation we had. I didn't do a fantastic job of hiding the fact that my sanity was hanging by a thread, and I knew he'd be worried about me. I could feel that I'd been the main reason he'd come. My brother had been worried about me, but there was more to his fears than that.

Now that I was able to feel the emotions he had inside, I felt his fear, anger, and insecurity. He hadn't wanted to come back here, and if it weren't for me, he wouldn't have.

* * * *

Ethan got out of his car and walked down to the longest pier, which overlooked the ocean. He hadn't told anyone that he was returning to town. He needed time to prepare for how he was going to explain his absence with little contact for five years to my parents, grandmother, and our mutual friends.

He was nervous about seeing everyone and thought that maybe a walk would calm his nerves. He didn't know what to say to everyone about why he had stayed away for so long. He knew that he couldn't tell anyone the real truth, part of which he couldn't even remember. I was the only one that could remember the whole truth, and I wished to God I couldn't.

I watched him run his hands through his hair, afraid that if they pushed him for answers, he'd reveal what he could remember about the secret he and I shared. It had stolen his life and left in its place constant worry and fear that what we'd done would be discovered. He wanted to scream out at the top of his lungs, but he didn't. Instead, he kept it hidden inside.

As he stood there, a chill went through his body, and he shivered. He'd forgotten how relentless the early spring wind could be in Sleepy Meadows.

What he didn't know was that I was in the wind, trying to make contact, trying to tell him that I was gone and that I was sorry for not just my suicide, but for the five years of hell he'd gone through because of me.

He shifted his gaze from the water and glanced towards an old familiar building on the dock that he'd known well. It was our parent's business: Hawkins' Fishing Company. It was a small business, but in a little town like Sleepy Meadows, it flourished.

Our father had always wanted Ethan to stay and work the family business, but things didn't work out that way. As he stood on the dock, he wondered what would've happened if he had stayed.

When he had left town, he had been 24-years-old and had lived a pretty sheltered life, just as I had. He had told our parents that he wanted to leave town and make his own way. Back then, he had thought that he had the total package to be a success. After all, he was six foot tall, good looking, fit, with blond hair and eyes that were deep blue. He had an appeal that was undeniable.

Unfortunately, he'd lost his confidence entirely in the time he'd been gone. The scar on his right cheek was a reminder of the past, of the secret events that connected the two of us forever.

The ocean reminded him of how much I'd enjoyed the water when we were kids. I used my newfound ability of thought transference to get him thinking about me as he stared out at the water sparkling in the moonlight.

He realized that being back in town rehashed memories and feelings that he had tried desperately to repress, even ones that had nothing to do with me.

He thought about his best friend, Kasey Menze, and what it would feel like to see him again. Ethan had never stopped thinking of him. He and Kasey had been inseparable growing up. Kasey had been like another older brother to me, but Ethan and Kasey had a different type of bond.

Sleepy Meadows was a small town, and it wouldn't be long before they ran into each other. He wondered what it would be like, what they would say that they hadn't already said. He didn't know what would happen, but he knew that it would be awkward.

Ethan put his hands in his pockets and walked slowly down the pier, heading back towards his car. Before getting inside, he looked up the hill toward the Wickcliff mansion.

I wondered if there was a way that he could see my spirit form in the window looking out. Although the mansion's dark presence was disturbing to him, he thought about coming up here and making sure I was alright, then leaving town again without letting anyone know he had come, especially Kasey. Maybe leaving before anyone saw him would save him from the unending questions from his family and friends.

He took in a deep breath, got into his car, put the key in the ignition, and glanced at the dashboard clock. It was almost ten o'clock. He had known it was late, but he didn't realize how late. He sighed, thinking that he'd just stay one night. He would say hello to our parents, check on me in the morning, and be on his way again. Where he would go after that didn't matter as long as it was far from Sleepy Meadows and his past.

As much as I wanted him to, my brother wasn't feeling my presence. I had to connect with someone else. I thought about our friend Kasey. He wasn't like anyone else. His mother always said when we were growing up that he had extraordinary gifts, believing he had psychic abilities. He confided in me once that he could see and hear things that others couldn't.

I couldn't believe that I hadn't thought about that before. I shifted my thoughts from my brother to concentrating on Kasey and feeling his presence.

If I were going to get through to anyone, it would be him.

Midnight's Edge, The Secrets of Sleepy Meadows

* * * *

On the main street of Sleepy Meadows, between several whitewashed clapboard storefronts stands a bar made of stone called The Hook. Kasey works there as a musician, singing at night on the small stage with his band he'd named Midnight's Edge.

When we were kids, Kasey's mother, Gracey, used to tell us stories and told us about ME. None of us kids had ever seriously believed it, but the idea that there was a time where the dead could come back to the land of the living always intrigued us. Now that I was dead and knew that Jeremy was planning to use ME to return to the mortal realm, I found myself wishing that I'd paid more attention to the stories. Maybe I would've known how to stop him if I just would've listened more closely instead of shrugging it off as an old wives tale.

Kasey was especially enamored with ME because his biological parents died when he was a baby. He'd fantasized that they would come back during ME and that their spirits would live again. When it never happened, Kasey lost faith in the legend, and it was a dream that fizzled out in childhood.

As Kasey came into focus in my mind, I saw him on the stage singing a song he had written for Ethan after he left. Kasey appeared pale as if he were ill. I wondered if maybe his abilities were telling him that I was in trouble or even that I had died, and that's why he looked sick.

I began to read his thoughts just as I had with Ethan moments before. He had indeed been feeling ill all day and had been thinking about me and Ethan for different reasons. He'd known that I was in trouble even before I knew what Jeremy had planned for me.

After the song was over, he kept his eyes closed and continued to hold his microphone, not wanting the thoughts he had of Ethan to end. Although Kasey had accepted Ethan's leaving, there was a time when he longed to find him. He almost thought about locating Ethan and following him to wherever he was. He would have if it weren't for having to take care of Gracey. Although she was still a feisty old woman, she'd grown dependent on him in her old age due to advanced arthritis and several other related aches and pains.

I felt the loneliness Kasey felt. I missed my brother too, even more now that I'd crossed over into a different realm. Knowing I'd never see him again, at least not in the way we'd been used to, saddened me.

If there was one benefit to what I'd done, it was that I now understood things I couldn't before, such as just how close Kasey and my brother had been and to what degree.

Although he had no idea about my suicide, Kasey sensed that something was wrong. The longer he stood there on the stage, the worse he felt. What disturbed him was that the psychic visions he had when he was younger always started out with the same queasy feeling in his stomach that he had now which always got worse and worse until he felt he no longer could stand it.

The crowd's applause waned, and he turned to his band members. "Let's take a break, guys. I'm not feeling so hot tonight."

Bucky Lorring, Kasey's drummer and the 19 year-old-son of the bar's owners, Hal and Shirley, patted him on the back noticing his pallid complexion. "Are you okay, Kase? You look pretty pale."

Kasey rubbed his forehead. "I'm fine. I might be coming down with something."

"You sure that's all it is? You look like you're about to faint or something."

"Yeah."

Bucky shrugged. "Okay, if you say so." He jumped off the stage and headed towards the bar.

Kasey wasn't sure if he sounded convincing and took in a deep breath. He felt his forehead. He noticed how hot and sweaty he'd become.

He placed the microphone back in the stand, held onto it and scanned the room. It was a slow night, and the customers didn't seem energetic. All he wanted to do was go home and curl up in bed.

As he let go of the microphone, he experienced a sudden, sharp, electric sensation in his head. His body stiffened, and he shut his eyes, trying to bear the pain. For a second, he held his breath and pinched the bridge of his nose, hoping to alleviate the pain, but the sensation persisted. He exhaled slowly attempting to regain his composure, but the tingling sensation continued over his whole body.

As his pain persisted, I realized that he was having some sort of psychic experience. This one had begun the same as one's he'd told me about when we were growing up. It started with him feeling ill and then he'd receive the tingling, painful sensation. This time, I felt like I was experiencing it with him.

He grabbed onto the microphone stand again, trying to balance himself. His neck stiffened, and another sensation pulsated through his body. His vision blurred, and it was as if I saw through his eyes.

He stepped forward awkwardly, knocking over the microphone stand and stumbling off the stage to the floor. He looked up, saw Bucky coming towards him, and gasped at the sight of him.

Bucky didn't look like the same young guy that Kasey and I had known. He now had cold, lifeless eyes and a sinister plastic grin on his face. Then the skin on his face sagged, and the bags under his eyes turned black and blue. His cheeks sank inward while his whole face turned blue, purple, and black as if his skin were rotting off his bones.

Then Bucky's eyeballs bulged and popped out of their sockets. Dead skin on Bucky's face fell off in clumps, his clothes rotted off his body, turning into a pile of dust on the floor. He'd morphed into a walking, living skeleton, and his remains moved closer to Kasey who backed up against the stage, his mouth agape. The smell of rotting flesh surrounded him.

I could see, feel and smell what was happening. The stench was as strong as it would've been had I been in the room with him. I wondered if my punishment for my suicide was that I'd be shown all of these terrible visions, desperately wanting to intervene but never being able to. I suddenly became lost in my thoughts, wondering if I'd be doomed to feel all the pain and suffering that my loved ones were experiencing and never be able to stop it.

I focused my attention back on Kasey. I saw him glance around the bar, seeing that all of the clientele had turned into skeletons just as Bucky had.

His heart beat faster, and I wondered if he'd be able to survive this. Sweat ran profusely down his face and neck. He wanted to get out of Bucky's path, but it was as if all his energy were gone. He couldn't move.

"What the hell's happening to me? This can't be real!"

He covered his face with his hands, desperate to shed the grotesque sight and the fear of not knowing what would happen next.

I wanted to scream out too, to tell him that he wasn't alone that I could see what he saw and that I was just as afraid. It was then that I heard a man's voice. It wasn't a voice that I had heard before, but yet it sounded strangely familiar. It wasn't coming from the bar; that much I could tell.

Kasey heard it too.

He searched the bar with his eyes, looking for the source. We then saw the image of an older man wearing a monk's cloak appear in front of us. He seemed familiar, but I had no idea from where I'd seen him and neither did Kasey.

The man was bald, and his eyes were a stunning blue. I continued to stare at him while Kasey shut his eyes. When he opened them, the man was still there. "Who are you?"

"I'm a friend," the strange man replied. "I can't explain our connection now."

"You aren't my friend. I don't know you. This must all be part of the illusion."

The man smiled warmly. "This isn't just an illusion, and I am your friend. In time, you'll see."

"Do you know what's happening to me?"

The man's smile faded. "I have something to show you."

Before Kasey could question him more, the man disappeared. In his place appeared the image of a cemetery and a large tomb. I recognized it immediately. The headstones were from the Wickcliff cemetery on the grounds near the mansion.

Kasey was jolted out of the vision when Bucky grabbed his arm.

"Kase, you alright?"

"Don't touch me!" He caught his breath when he realized that Bucky looked like himself again.

"What the hell's the matter?" Bucky extended his hand. "Let me help you up."

He was apprehensive at first then managed a half smile of relief.

"Come on, Kase." Bucky put his hand out further. "You obviously can't stand on your own."

He took Bucky's hand and stood up, noticing that everyone around him appeared to be normal again too.

"Who were you talking to just now?" Bucky asked. "You were talking to someone, but it wasn't me. You were looking right past me as if you could see through me."

He gazed at Bucky blankly. "Huh?"

Hal, Bucky's dad, approached and put his hand on his shoulder. "What just happened?"

"I don't know for sure." He glanced around the room. "I just felt faint, I guess. I haven't felt well today."

Regardless of what Kasey said, I knew the truth, even though he had no intention of telling them what he saw. He didn't even understand it himself, and he knew he couldn't explain it even if he wanted to. They'd think he was crazy if he tried.

Hal told his wife, Shirley, who was now behind the bar, to call a doctor.

Kasey gripped Hal's arm and then eyed Shirley. "No. I'm fine. I didn't sleep last night, and I haven't eaten today." He forced a smile. "That's not a good combo, you know. I just need to go home and get some sleep."

Hal's eyes narrowed. "You do that. Christ, you gave us a real scare." He turned to the crowd who had huddled around them and put his hands up. "Everything's alright, folks. There's nothing more to see here."

The crowd went back to their seats slowly, buzzing about what had just happened. Hal walked back to the bar.

"Let me help you get your balance," Bucky said, giving Kasey his arm.

Kasey grabbed onto him. "Thanks. I'm sorry I scared you and your folks. But I'll be fine."

"I don't think you are." Bucky paused. "You didn't answer my question. You were talking to someone who wasn't there."

"I've felt peculiar all night like I told you. I guess I'm exhausted."

Bucky took his hand off Kasey's arm and nodded. "Yeah, it's strange, but I feel the same way. There's been an odd feeling in here all night. Everyone's had the energy of a wet rag." He chuckled. "I think you just woke everyone up, though."

Kasey stood up straight and laughed. "I guess I did."

Bucky walked away, got a bottle of water from the bar, and gave it to him. "Here, take this and go out and get some fresh air. That always helps me when I don't feel well."

Bucky patted his arm and walked away again. Kasey sighed, opened the bottle, and took a sip. The water drizzled down his chin, and he wiped it off his goatee. He raised the bottle to his forehead to cool himself down and rubbed it over his dark hair, now sopping wet.

The vision was the strongest, most intense one he'd ever had. The last five years without a vision that he'd spent trying to build a normal life were shattered. Instead, he felt the same fear, the same loneliness, and the same isolation that he felt growing up.

He raised the bottle to his lips again, hoping that the water would help cool him down and relieve the feeling of dread that he had in the pit of his stomach. He grabbed his coat by the door and walked outside.

Another swig of the water helped clear his throat. For a brief second, he wished it were beer, remembering the taste and how it had made him feel. He'd quit drinking long ago and had been sober for many years. He hadn't even thought about drinking for a long time. This latest vision reminded him of why he had started drinking in the first place. Alcohol had been the only thing that made his visions stop. He had depended on it so that he could function. It wasn't until he realized that he had to kill his habit before it killed him that he quit.

He looked down the vacant street and saw the fog rolling in from the ocean, coming in thick as if something cold, dead, and lifeless were encroaching. The thought made him shiver.

In the sky, the moon demanded his attention. He stared as it forced its way out from behind the clouds. It drew him in immediately, and for a brief second his eyes were transfixed as he saw a skull morph onto the surface of the moon. The vision vanished as quickly as it appeared.

"Not again," he said, walking into the alleyway. "Why is this happening?"

Chapter 4

"Why is what happening?"

Kasey turned around quickly. An unknown figure stood around the corner of the building in the dark. He couldn't see who it was at first until the person walked out into the dim moonlight.

He was relieved to see that it was only Reed Withers, the son of the town's Sheriff, Graham. Reed, who was about five years younger than Kasey, was tall and thin with reddish-brown hair and ice-blue eyes.

"Sorry, I didn't mean to startle you," Reed said. "You look like you've seen a ghost. You alright?"

"I just wanted to be by myself for a little while. What are you doing here?"

"I was looking for you."

"Well, you found me." He paused. "Look, I don't mean to be rude, but I was hoping to have some time alone."

Reed put his hands up. "I'm sorry I interrupted whatever's going on here. It was nice seeing you." He turned to walk away.

Kasey stopped him. "Reed, please wait."

Reed turned back around and faced him.

Kasey exhaled. "I'm sorry if I sounded short. I'm not feeling well."

"You don't look so well either. Forgive me for saying so, but you look terrible."

He wiped his forehead with the back of his hand. "Thanks a lot."

"Sorry, but it's freezing out here, and you're sweating. Do you think you have a fever?" Reed reached out to touch him.

He pushed Reed's hand away and stepped back. "Leave me alone."

"Geez, Kase. What the hell's wrong with you? Is this why you didn't make it to my place the other night?"

He shook his head. "No. Something came up. I'm sorry."

Reed approached him again, putting a hand on his arm. "I just expected a phone call is all. Maybe you can make it up to me when you're feeling better."

He pushed Reed's hand away again. "What's happening now is way more important."

"I'll ask again. What's happening?"

"Hell if I know. But I'm going to find out."

Reed exhaled swiftly and rolled his eyes. He stood there for a moment in silence, his face illuminated in the moonlight. Kasey watched as Reed's face began to morph into a skeleton just like Bucky's had before in the bar.

Kasey gasped and backed up quickly. "No! Not again!"

Reed's eye sockets were hollow, and flesh hung from his bones. His teeth had become green and yellowed. He stepped closer to Kasey, his voice lower, guttural. "What's wrong? Don't like the sight of me, Kase?" He cackled.

Kasey backed up further. "Stay away from me!"

There was a flash of light that passed in front of Kasey's eyes. Reed's appearance returned to normal in an instant.

Reed glared at him, his voice back to normal. "Why are you acting this way? First, you blow me off the other night and now this. What the hell's going on?"

"I just want to be left alone," Kasey said, putting his hand up. "I'm going through something that I can't explain. Will you please leave?"

Reed huffed and stepped back. "I don't even know why I bother." He stomped away and disappeared into the night.

The back door of the bar swung open, and Shirley came out, putting her hand over her heart. "Oh, Kasey, I didn't realize you were out here."

"I needed some air."

"Thank God it's only you, I don't want Hal to see me smoking." She reached into her purse and pulled out a cigarette. She looked back behind her like she was expecting Hal to catch her in the act. "Can I borrow a light?"

"You know I don't smoke," he said, agitated. "Didn't you quit?"

"Shush. I don't want Hal to hear. You know he's always riding me about quitting." She looked at him more closely. "Are you feeling any better? You gave us quite a scare."

They were disrupted by sirens and watched an ambulance speed past.

"Wonder what that's all about," she said, searching her purse for a light. "It's getting so late. I guess there's no timetable for people in crisis."

I wondered if the sirens had anything to do with me. But that was impossible. No one had found me in the attic yet. Had someone gotten concerned when they couldn't reach me and called for help? That couldn't have been it. I'd been so reclusive lately that it wouldn't surprise people if I vanished. They'd just think I'd gone off into my own little world.

I concentrated as intensely as I could for Kasey to hear me. If he could see these horrific visions, and if he could see and hear a man that neither of us knew, why couldn't he hear me?

"Kasey, it's me, Shelly. I'm with you. I've crossed over, and I need your help."

Kasey's eyes brightened, and he mumbled. "Those sirens have something to do with Ethan. Someone he loves is in trouble. I have to go see my mother."

I did it! Now he was starting to get it. I'd been right thinking I could get through to him.

Shirley gave him a peculiar look. "What did you say?"

He turned to her. "Nothing. I gotta go. I'll see you later."

"Feel better!" she yelled after him as he dashed off.

* * * *

I watched as Kasey got on his motorcycle and headed towards his mother's house. He hoped Gracey could help explain why he had these visions and feelings of dread.

Gracey wasn't like everyone else. When Kasey had first confided in her about his abilities, she not only believed him, but she encouraged him to continue to fine tune his abilities and make them stronger. Although he never wanted to, he continued to see things anyway. She would comfort him as a child and explain that he was exceptional and that he'd been given his gift to do marvelous things.

He was confused and scared now and needed the comfort and reassurance of his mother, the only one who would understand.

What confused him the most was that his visions stopped several years ago around the time that Ethan left town. He was sure that he'd never have to deal with them again and had been grateful. Not only were they back, they were more vivid than ever.

As he turned a corner, he thought about the feeling he had at The Hook when he saw the ambulance go by, and that it had something to do with Ethan or someone close to him.

He didn't realize it yet, but I was slowly starting to break through to him.

He pulled into Gracey's driveway, ran to the door, and used his key to open it and go inside. He found her still awake, sitting in her favorite chair in front of the TV. Her Boston Terrier, Scruffy, jumped off of her lap and greeted him.

She put her hand over her heart. "Kasey, it's so late. You gave me a start. I didn't expect that anyone would be coming in here this late. I thought you might have been a burglar or something."

"I'm sorry, Mom," he said, approaching her. "I have to talk to you."

She turned down the volume on the TV. "Did you hear those sirens a bit ago? They about did me in. I don't know how much this old heart of mine can take."

He glanced at her kind face, realizing how tired and frail she looked.

She was an extremely strong-willed, determined woman who had raised him as a single parent. Roles had been reversed in recent years between them. Her mind and will had remained strong, but her body had begun to betray her. Her joints were racked with arthritis, her gait had become unsteady, and she rarely was able to walk more than a few feet without her cane.

He had to take care of her and knew that one day she wouldn't be there for him to lean on in times like these. That thought scared him more than any vision ever could.

"Did you get that same bad feeling that I did when you heard the sirens?" she asked. "I'm sorry to say that this just isn't any normal night. I can't shake the feeling that something's terribly wrong. That's why I'm still awake. I couldn't sleep."

"I think something's wrong too. That's what I wanted to talk to you about." He knelt down and put his hand on her knee. "I've been having a rough night, even before the sirens started."

She touched his face tenderly with her wrinkled hand. "Rough night? You haven't had a drink, have you?"

"Nothing like that. It's the visions…they've started again, this time much worse."

Her face tightened. "I was afraid that this would happen again someday. What did you see?"

He stood up and ran his hands through his brown hair. "Bucky, Reed, and some of the bar patrons decayed in front of my face. All I saw were their skeletons. It was horrible." He paused, rubbed his temples, and then put his arms back down. "Wait a minute. Did you just say you were afraid of that? You knew that they'd start again?"

Her eyes lowered. "I suspected as much."

"But you told me you thought they'd stopped for good."

"You were younger. I didn't want to scare you. You had so many problems with your drinking. It was wishful thinking, I suppose, for your sake that is." She sighed. "Your real mother had visions all through her adult life right up until the day she died. She was so convinced that something was going to happen to you if you stayed with her that she asked me to look after you."

He brushed a strand of her salt and pepper hair back and kissed her on the forehead. "As far as I'm concerned, you're my real mother."

She took his hand. "I know darling. I'm talking about your biological mother. If the visions have started again, it must mean that something's about to happen. We have to figure out what it is before it's too late."

She tried to get up, but he put his hands on her arms. "Whoa. Don't get yourself all excited. You need to rest. You don't get along as well as you used to."

She tried again. "I'm fine."

"No, you aren't." He got her to sit back. "I can always tell when your leg's bothering you. You should know better by now."

His phone rang, interrupting them. He got his phone out of his pocket and looked at the caller ID. It was Shirley at the bar. She told him that something had happened to my dad.

The sirens had nothing to do with me, but they were for my dad. With everything that had happened, I'd forgotten that I'd spoken to him earlier.

I'd been hysterical on the phone with him and had told him for the first time that I'd been hearing Jeremy's voice, and that he'd been taunting me. Dad may not have believed me about the voices, but he knew I needed help. Now I remembered that he'd been on his way to see me and hadn't made it. I wanted to know what had happened to my father.

Kasey closed his phone and glanced at Gracey, still seated in her chair, staring at him.

"What happened?" she asked. "I can't take much more suspense."

"That was Shirley on the phone. Jeffrey Hawkins had a heart attack."

She gasped. "Is he—?"

"He's alive, but she didn't know much about his condition."

She reached for the phone on the table next to her chair and picked it up. "I have to call Carol."

He moved towards the door, put his hand on the knob and turned his head around to face his mom. "I'll go to the hospital and see what I can find out. I'll call you soon."

"Kasey, please promise me you'll be careful out there." She wore a worried expression on her face. "My feelings aren't clear. I don't know what's going to happen. All I know is that whatever it is could be dangerous for you."

He gave her a perplexed look. He didn't have time to ask her what that meant. He was more concerned about my dad, and so was I.

"Don't worry, Mom. I'll be fine. I just want to make sure that Ethan's family's alright."

He stepped outside and shut the door behind him, zipped up his coat, and went down the porch steps. He got on his bike again and started it. Any fears that he had about his visions or confusion over what happened had now subsided.

All he thought about now was that Ethan would be coming back to Sleepy Meadows because of our dad. He wondered what would happen when he came face-to-face with his best friend again.

* * * *

Ethan's heart sank as he pulled up to our parent's house. He wasn't ready to look them in the eye and lie to their faces about why he'd left Sleepy Meadows. He couldn't let them know how worried he was about me. He had to convince them that he just came into town for a short visit and hoped that they wouldn't question the late hour. They could never find out the secret that we shared.

He pulled into the driveway next to our grandmother's car and thought she must be there alone because he didn't see either one of our parent's cars. He thought that odd for this hour. They should all be at home and asleep by now.

He turned the car off and peered into the living room window seeing that the light was still on. Since Gram was still up, he figured that he might as well go in. He went up to the door and knocked, playing with his jacket collar while he waited for an answer. After a moment, he heard footsteps approaching the door and it opened revealing Gram.

Ethan smiled at her and stretched out his arms. "Surprise," he said, not knowing what else to say.

She appeared confused. "Ethan? What are you doing here?"

He dropped his arms and his smile. "That wasn't exactly the greeting I expected."

"Sorry, but I didn't know you were—"

"Aren't you happy to see me, Gram?"

"Of course, dear." She stepped aside, letting him enter the house, shut the door behind him and managed a half-smile as she gave him a peck on the cheek. "I'm just surprised. How did you know?"

He gave her a confused expression. "Know what?"

"Your mother must've gotten a hold of you somehow. How on earth did you get here so quickly?"

"I haven't talked to Mom. My coming here was supposed to be a surprise. What's going on here?"

"You mean you really don't know?"

"I just decided to come for a visit. It's been a long time, Gram."

Her eyes lowered. "Five years. I know that darling. So this is just a coincidence?"

"Will you just cut to the chase? The suspense is killing me. And where are my parents?" He scanned the room but found no one else.

"I've tried getting in touch with you this evening. I called your friend Becca because she'd said that she'd talked to you recently. I told your mother I'd keep trying you. That's why I'm still here. I was trying to track you down before I went to be with them."

He swallowed, realizing for the first time how shaken up she was. "What's wrong, Gram? What's happened?"

She went through the entryway leading to the living room with him following her. She motioned to the couch. "Why don't you sit down? I have some grim news."

He sat, and she sat beside him, putting put her hand on his knee. "Your parents are at the hospital."

A lump formed in his throat. "Is it Shelly? Is she okay?"

She blinked and leaned back. "Shelly? Why would you think this is about her?"

"No reason. I'm just eliminating some of the possibilities."

"I've been trying to reach her too. She isn't answering. But she usually doesn't up in that place." She paused, locking eyes with him. "Something happened between you two at the Wickcliff mansion, didn't it? That's why you left five years ago."

He froze. "No."

She squeezed his arms. "You can tell me. It had to do with Rory's death, didn't it? You were there with Shelly when he killed himself. Ever since then everything's changed. You left us, and Shelly became a recluse."

He looked away. "I don't want to talk about this right now."

"Something did happen. Something you're not telling us."

He faced her again. "That's not relevant now. Just please tell me what's happened."

She put her hand on his shoulder. "It's your father. He's had a heart attack."

His chest tightened. "Is he—?"

"He's alive."

He exhaled quickly. Relieved, he got up and headed towards the door. He turned back to Gram. "What the hell are we waiting for then? Let's get to the hospital."

Chapter 5

When Ethan and Gram arrived at the hospital, he went immediately to the information desk and found out that Dad was in ICU. He felt like he couldn't get there fast enough, like the ground was made of quicksand.

In the ICU family waiting room, he found our mother, Carol, standing alone. She turned around at the sound of his voice. Her worried expression lightened when she saw his face.

They hadn't parted on the best terms when he'd left, and he didn't know how she was going to react to him being home. I never understood the problems in their relationship, but now I had a better understanding. He and Mom were alike. They were both secretive, and their feelings ran deep.

He noticed that she hadn't changed much since the last time he saw her. Her hair was still dark and short, and her eyes were just as blue as his. She was just as beautiful as she'd always been.

She looked at him for a moment before touching his face. "Ethan, you're really here?"

"I'm sorry. I didn't mean to startle you."

She embraced him. "What are you doing here? You couldn't have known. None of us could reach you."

"I decided to come for a visit. I didn't expect this."

"Oh, Ethan...I'm so glad you're home."

After a moment, he broke the embrace and looked into her eyes. "What's going on with Dad?"

"It was a major heart attack."

"When did this happen?"

"A few hours ago as best I can tell. I went out for groceries earlier this evening, and when I came home, he was gone. He left me a note saying that he was going out. That's all it said. I found out later that he was going up to the Wickcliff mansion."

"He was? Why?"

"He must've been going to see Shelly. His car was found near Lover's Bluff. He must've suffered the attack on the way. A passerby saw his car on the side of the road, in the ditch, and called an ambulance."

I felt immense guilt. My father had a heart attack on the way to see me. It had been my behavior that had upset him. I was likely to have caused his attack.

Ethan's throat tightened. "He's going to make it, right?"

"I don't know." Mom's eyes drifted to the floor. "I hope he'll pull through."

"You hope?"

Her eyes raised and met his. "Of course."

His facial expression soured. "You don't seem all that concerned about him, and, by the tone of your voice, it sounds like you could be talking about a stranger."

Her head went back. "You asked me a question, and I answered it. What else do you want me to say? Of course I want your dad to be alright."

He exhaled sharply and looked away. "Could've fooled me."

Gram, who had been standing behind them, got between them. "Stop it! We haven't seen you for years, Ethan. You have no right to talk to your mother that way."

"I agree," Mom said.

"This isn't the time or the place for you to start your nonsense," Gram said. "You both need to focus on Jeffrey."

Ethan glanced at Mom and sighed. "I'm sorry, I shouldn't have said that. I'm just worried."

Mom touched his arm gently. "Your grandmother's right. We have to put our differences aside. It's been too long since I've seen you for us to fight." She turned to Gram. "Mom, did you get in touch with Shelly yet?"

Gram shook her head. "I haven't been able to get her."

Ethan pulled out his cell phone. "I'll go outside and try to call her."

Mom grabbed his arm. "You look exhausted. Where have you been?"

"I can't talk about it right now. I just need some air. I'll let you know if I get in touch with her."

He raced down the hall and through the main doors of the hospital. He felt trapped inside. Once outside, he looked up at the sky and exhaled. The air was like ice and made him shiver.

He opened his phone to call me, but before he could even dial, he heard a familiar voice from behind him.

"Hey, stranger."

He turned around and met eyes with Kasey. They stood silently gazing at each other for a moment.

It was Kasey who finally broke the ice and gave him a hug. "You look good, Ethan."

"So do you, Kase."

"I can't believe that you're here. I wasn't sure if I'd ever see you again."

"I guess I came home just in time, huh?" Ethan chuckled sarcastically. "I told my father when I left that I didn't want to die here like he was going to, and now I'm back just in time to watch it happen."

"Don't talk like that. You don't know what's happening yet."

Ethan turned his back on him and gazed up at the sky. "I'm a terrible son. I never appreciated anything that he did for me. I left my family, and I was gone for so long. I just hope that I get the chance to tell him how sorry I am."

Kasey touched his shoulder. "You will."

Ethan turned around to face him, and his eyes softened. "It's good to see you, Kase, regardless of the circumstances."

Kasey pulled him into another embrace. Ethan tensed up at first, but then let Kasey hug him for a brief moment before breaking the embrace.

"Are you alright, Ethan?"

"I'm fine. How did you know to come here?"

"Shirley told me about your dad, and I hoped you'd be here once you knew. I didn't expect to see you this soon, though. How did you know?"

"I didn't know about dad. I was just coming for a visit."

Kasey raised his chin. "If he hadn't been here and if I hadn't run into you here, would you've told me you were in town?"

Ethan's eyes drifted away, giving Kasey his answer without him saying anything.

"I see." Kasey stepped back. "I thought that we were at least still friends, if nothing else."

Ethan met his gaze again. "We are Kase. Things are complicated."

"Why haven't you called, emailed, something? You've been gone for five years. What happened to you? What did I do to make you leave?"

Ethan shifted his stance uncomfortably. "You? You didn't do anything. It was me."

"That doesn't explain much. Why would you leave your home and family, your friends, me? I have to ask this, did it have to do with Rory's suicide?"

Ethan put his hand up. "I can't get into this with you right now. I need to find my sister and tell her about Dad. Shelly doesn't know yet. Have you seen her lately?"

"No. I never see her. No one does."

Ethan turned away from Kasey again this time glancing into the hospital's glass doors. "I can't take this waiting. I just need to know something, no matter what the outcome."

Kasey put a hand on his shoulder. "If there's anything I can do—"

"I've gotta contact Shelly somehow."

"I'll help you find her."

"No!"

Kasey jumped back, surprised by Ethan's sharp tone. "Fine."

"I'm sorry," Ethan said, softening his tone. "There isn't anything you can do. I just need to be with my family now."

"I was just trying to help. I didn't mean to upset you."

"I know you didn't. I didn't mean to snap at you like that. I'm just on edge right now and frustrated that we can't find Shelly."

"I get it."

Ethan and Kasey turned when they heard footsteps approaching them. It was their childhood friend, Rebecca Bowen, smiling widely.

"Is there room for one more," she said, "or is this a private party?" She pulled Ethan into a hug. "How ya doing, kiddo?"

Ethan broke the embrace and looked at her smiling. She hadn't changed at all. She was still the attractive, girl-next-door type, with long, soft brown hair and eyes to match.

"I'm okay," he said. "Now that I'm back with friends like you."

Kasey shifted his feet and said nothing.

Rebecca raised an eyebrow. "Really? Even with your father in the hospital?"

"Okay. I'm not so glad about that."

She lost her smile. "I figured as much."

"Thanks for coming. Gram told me she called you."

"Brynn called me too. She volunteers at the hospital now and heard that your dad was admitted."

"Little Brynn?"

Rebecca chuckled. "My little sister isn't so little anymore. Five years is a long time." She turned her attention to Kasey. "Hey, Kase, you haven't said a word."

Kasey barely made eye contact with her. "Hey, Becca."

Her eyes shot back and forth between them. "Why do I have the feeling I'm interrupting something? I thought you two would be happy to see each other after all this time. Instead, you both look miserable."

"You aren't interrupting anything," Ethan said. "Kase and I were just talking."

"That's right," Kasey said, and then glanced down at his watch. "It's getting late. I should probably go. I'm not needed here."

"Kase..." Ethan began.

Rebecca exhaled. "What's that supposed to mean?"

"Good to see you Ethan, Becca," Kasey said. He pushed past Ethan and headed towards the parking lot.

Rebecca watched him leave and then turned to Ethan. "Now I know I interrupted something. If it were any chillier between you two—"

Ethan waved his hand. "I don't want to talk about Kase right now. I want to hear all about what's going on in your life."

She shrugged. "Oh, you know, same old thing different day."

He chuckled. "Right. I don't believe that. Have you come to your senses and dumped Mr. Perfect yet?"

She rolled her eyes. "Pit Bowen? Who me? Why in the world would I want to do that? He's a brash, arrogant, self-centered, disgusting, poor excuse for a man. What woman would want to give all that up?"

He laughed. "I have to admit I never understood it. My mom always wanted us together you know."

"Don't start. You could've had all this."

He put his arm around her and smiled. "Same old Becca."

"What? You asked, and I told you."

He tightened his arm around her. "I missed you."

"You could've called a girl more often, you big jerk."

He pulled away and put his hands up. "I know, I know. I suck as a friend."

Her expression turned more serious. "You still haven't told me why you left and why you haven't come back since. You belong here, Ethan. This is your home."

He raised an eyebrow. "I don't know where I belong."

"Tell me what's been going on with you. Help me understand."

He looked away. "Things haven't been easy."

"I know the feeling." She embraced him again. "I missed you too. It's nice to have you home. It wasn't the same without you." After a moment, she stepped back and took his hand. "Now come on. I'm sure that we both could use some good news so let's go get some."

They both walked towards the entrance to the hospital. Ethan stopped and held up his finger.

"One sec," he said, pulling his phone out and dialing my number. There was no answer again. He glanced at Rebecca. "Where the hell is she? She doesn't even know about Dad."

She shrugged. "I assume you're talking about Shelly. Honestly, Ethan, I wouldn't know. All I know about her is what I hear in town and told you on the phone the other day. I hardly see her anymore. Nobody does. She never comes down from that stone prison on the hill."

"That's what Kase said. Is that true? Never?"

"Ever since you left it's been that way. The rumor in town is that there's some deep, dark secret up there in that house that she doesn't want anyone to discover, and that's why she never leaves. You know all the rumors about that place. I suppose I don't blame her after what happened to Rory—"

He grabbed her arms tightly. "Please don't say that again, ever."

She pushed away from him. "What did I say?" She cocked her head. "What haven't you told me, Ethan? Do you know why she never leaves? Did you leave because of what happened to Rory?"

"No." Ethan inhaled and then smiled nervously. "I'm sorry. I'm a wreck. We'd better get back inside. It's cold out here, and I need to see my father." He turned sharply and began to walk inside.

Chapter 6

Rebecca followed him knowing that there was something deeply wrong with my brother. She was right of course. There was something wrong with him, more than just our father's condition.

I was the only one who knew that it involved our secret. Not even my brother knew the whole truth about what happened the night Rory died. He believed he was protecting me, but the truth was that Jeremy's tricks had deceived both of us. I knew what happened that night. In time, Ethan would remember.

That wasn't crucial right now, though. I stopped thinking about Ethan and thought about Kasey again, hoping to make contact. He had begun to feel my presence. I had to get through.

I found Kasey hurrying towards the hospital parking lot. He wasn't sure if it were just the cold, or his encounter with Ethan that made him feel chilled to the bone.

Seeing Ethan again was an emotional experience for him. They had been close once, how close I'd not known until now. Then one day he was gone. It hurt Kasey that his best friend had never bothered to keep in touch, and it felt worse when Ethan snapped at him when he was just trying to help.

Kasey stopped walking, breathed in the night air and exhaled deeply. He wondered why he had even bothered after all this time. Then he realized how selfish he was being. *Ethan's here for his father, not for me.*

The uncomfortable meeting was the last thing he had wanted to happen. He needed a place to clear his head. He got on his motorcycle and drove to Lover's Bluff, a place that overlooked the ocean on a winding road that led to the Wickcliff mansion. The bluff was where he often went to listen to the waves crashing on the rocks below. The sound had a calming effect on him when he was upset, much like it had for my brother.

At the bluff, he approached the ledge with his hands in his jean pockets. As he looked out into the distance and listened to the waves crashing, he took in a deep breath and closed his eyes.

He thought about the legend he'd heard when he was young about a married couple who were members of the Wickcliff family. Supposedly, they were killed one night when their car hit the winding curve near the bluff too fast. Their car had fallen into the ocean killing them both.

It was rumored that they'd been drinking too much. Some others said that they were fighting. No matter what the cause of the crash, their bodies were never recovered. He even remembered their names: Jeremy Wickcliff and his wife, Lucy.

He didn't know for sure if the story were true or not. But, he had always wondered who they were and what they were doing that night. The legend always made him think about his biological parents and why they had to die. Why it wasn't meant for him to know them.

The moon peered through the fog, and he stared up at it, half expecting to see the skull appear in it as it had earlier in the evening. This time all he saw was the moonlight glistening on the silver waves below.

After he he'd waited there for a few minutes, the feeling of dread that he had earlier in the evening came back to him. He shivered and zipped up his coat.

Even here, he couldn't seem to shake the feeling that something else was wrong. There was only one thing that used to help with the visions, help with the fear. He needed a drink. It was when he drank that the visions would subside.

Maybe if I have just one...

No. That wasn't an option for him anymore. He'd worked too hard at his sobriety to go back. There had to be another way. Although the temptation was there, he'd been sober for long enough to know that he couldn't go back to that dark place. He'd proven to himself that he didn't need it.

He pulled out his cell phone and glanced at the clock. It was late, and the emotions of the night were getting the best of him. He thought he might as well go home. There was no point in staying here.

Before leaving, he glanced up at the mansion, monstrous and black, foreboding, looming over him and the town like a black raven on its perch.

There were only a few lights on. He noticed one coming from a window on the very top. It was the attic where my spirit stood peering out the window.

He'd never seen that light on before, and assumed it had to be the attic. For a fleeting moment, he thought he saw someone standing there and wondered who could be up there this late at night. He knew that the only other person who lived there besides me and the servants was Irma Wickcliff. She was in her nineties, and he knew she wouldn't be awake now.

I wondered if I'd done it. I wondered if I'd been able to make contact with him and wondered if he saw me. As he stared up at the window, I opened my eyes and called out, flailing my arms. He had to have seen me. He was looking right at me.

I knew that since he knew it couldn't be Irma in the attic that he figured it was me. He thought that since I couldn't be reached to be told about my dad, he'd come up here and tell me in person. He still didn't realize that I was dead, but I was getting closer to making contact.

I harvested every ounce of energy I had into connecting with him. It had to be him. He's the only one who had the ability to see and hear me.

As he continued to stare at the window, he felt a sharp, pulsating sensation in his head, almost like a severe migraine headache. He grabbed both sides of his head with his hands, groaned, and fell to one knee.

As the pain continued, he finally heard me. I'd finally gotten through.

"Help me. Help me, Kasey."

His pain subsided quickly, and he got back on his feet. He stared back up at the window hoping to see me again. This time there was no one. It was clear to him what his visions meant now. I was in trouble, and he had to make sure I was okay before it was too late.

* * * *

"Hurry, Kasey," I said aloud, staring out the window of the attic at him, knowing that he no longer could hear or see me. I was out of his thoughts and back in my spirit body again.

I turned back around when I heard Jeremy laughing in the background. He appeared in the painting again.

"There's no more hope or help for you," he said. "I'd love to stay and chat, but I've got plans for tonight. I'm being reborn in the body of another during Midnight's Edge, and you get to see it happen."

That's when the door of the attic opened, and Gaul entered. He was large and intimidating, no ordinary man by any means. The Wickcliffs kept his origins a secret when I was alive, but now I knew that he was a ghoul, an emotionless slave to the Wickcliffs, neither happy nor sad about Jeremy's imminent return.

Suddenly Gaul's past came flooding into my mind. He'd been enslaved by the Wickcliffs centuries ago but was most recently a servant to Jeremy's father, Harold, and his grandfather, Pierre, when they had been alive.

His connection with the family went back to the beginning of his existence—a tale of death and rebirth—when Pierre, Jeremy's grandfather, extracted his soul from the dark realm, a realm of demons and evil spirits.

Jeremy's family had created Gaul for the purpose of him being their servant forever. Gaul's function was and always had been to protect their family—the living and the dead. To watch over them at all times. He was made to be the eyes and ears of the Wickcliff mansion and to protect not only those who lived there but their cemetery and mausoleum.

He'd been around long enough to have served several generations. He'd been created to be a cold, unfeeling being, with no will of his own. The only desire he was supposed to possess was to serve the Wickcliffs. Because of them, their blood ran through his ghoulish veins, and he had no choice but to obey their every whim. He was a servant and nothing else.

Even though I was dead, his presence frightened me. He approached my body still hanging from the rafters and stared at it with no feeling or remorse.

"You know what needs to be done," Jeremy said, behind him. "Take care of the body."

It was true what Jeremy had said earlier. Gaul was helping him. He could hear Jeremy from the ghost realm.

Gaul nodded slowly, then rotated on his heel and left the attic without uttering a word.

I screamed out his name, but he didn't hear me. My attempt to get his attention only entertained Jeremy more.

"It's useless," he said. "No one can hear you. You aren't strong enough to get through."

The door closed and once again, I was a prisoner here with Jeremy. I had to shut him out. I needed Kasey to realize that I was dead, and that could only happen if I connected with him again.

* * * *

Kasey arrived at the mansion, parked his bike near some bushes by the family cemetery and walked up to the door. As he knocked, he thought about what he'd say to whoever answered the door.

He wondered how he'd explain his visit at such a late hour. He realized that they'd probably think he was crazy, but he didn't care. I knew that he'd seen me moments before and that he was worried about me. He was going to be just as devastated as my family when he found out what I'd done, and I felt sorry for him.

He'd been so lost in his thoughts about what happened to me that he almost hadn't noticed that no one had come to the door yet. Figuring that everyone was in bed and that I couldn't hear him, he went around to the back of the house hoping to find another way in. He couldn't be positive that he wasn't being watched, so he remained crouched down to remain out of sight.

He got to the back door, tugged on it, and realized that it was locked up just as tightly as the front door. I saw him turn around to leave, but I couldn't let him go. He was too close to me now. I mustered as much strength as I could and called out to him.

"*Kasey...*"

He turned around. He'd heard me again. My voice came through like a whisper in the wind. I wasn't strong enough yet to get my voice through any louder, but at least I was getting through to him.

"Who is it?" he asked softly. "Who's calling me?"

He looked up at the window as he'd done down by the bluff just a little while before. I'd hoped that he would see me in the window as he had before, but this time he saw nothing.

"Kasey, you have to listen to me. There isn't much time..."

It took a moment for him to realize that it was my voice. "Shelly? Where are you? Are you alright? Your family's been trying to reach you for hours."

He hit the door with his fist. He was thinking about me, and now he could hear me. We had enough of a connection for me to communicate with him more clearly. With all the willpower I could muster, I commanded his attention and made him see what I saw.

He began to feel light headed and groaned, rubbing his temple. When he looked up, he was no longer outside, but he was inside the mansion. He saw a light at the end of a hallway illuminating the narrow set of stairs that led to the attic although he didn't know where they led yet.

As he began to approach the stairs, he felt frightened. He needed to know where the stairs led, and he needed to know what was going on. I could tell that the fear paralyzed him. He believed that what he was seeing was only in his mind, and that scared him the most.

I could feel his rapid heartbeat; I could hear his intensified breathing. I hadn't meant to scare him. I just needed him to find out the truth.

"This isn't real," he said, stopping before he reached the stairs. "I know that this is only a vision. I'm not afraid."

Saying the words didn't make them any truer. He wasn't afraid of the visions as much as he was afraid that he'd be lost inside his mind forever.

With one final deep breath, he approached the bottom of the staircase. When he got there, he heard a door creaking at the top of the steps. It sounded as if it were opening.

He didn't want to go up, but he didn't have a choice. Much like Jeremy had forced my mortal body up into the attic earlier, I discovered that I was able to do the same thing to Kasey using my newfound abilities. If he could find me and see me, I could warn him about Jeremy's plan.

He put his hand on the hand rail leading up the stairs. It felt cold to the touch. "Shelly, are you there?"

Although I tried, I couldn't answer him. I started to think about him finding my body.

Having heard my footsteps above him, he climbed the stairs calling out. "I'm coming, Shelly."

He reached the landing and saw that the door was slightly ajar. He opened it the whole way. At first, he saw nothing but old furniture covered in dust and cobwebs. He saw a chair turned on its side and then looked up. He gasped when he saw me hanging from a rope. He tried to reach out to me, but as fast as he had entered the vision he came out of it.

I hadn't been strong enough to maintain contact for that long. I was so close to being able to tell him the truth! When would I ever be strong enough to? Would I ever be able to get out of here? As much as I tried not to, I was beginning to lose hope.

Kasey found himself back on the lawn having snapped out of his vision, screaming, his heart pounding. He couldn't accept that he'd just seen me dead. He stumbled away from the mansion and got no more than a few feet before he collapsed.

Chapter 7

Realizing that I couldn't do anything to get through to Kasey now that he was unconscious, I focused my attention back on my brother. At least maybe I could find out what was going on with Dad.

I watched as Ethan walked back into the waiting room of the hospital with Rebecca behind him. It was there that they found Mom.

"Any news, Mom?" he asked.

She didn't make eye contact with him. "None, I'm afraid."

"What the hell's taking so long? Why won't they tell us anything?"

She laid her hand on his shoulder. "They're doing all they can." She noticed Rebecca behind him. "Hello, Becca. Thank you for coming."

"Of course, Mrs. Hawkins," Rebecca said. "Is there anything I can do?"

"You can call me Carol."

Rebecca smiled. "I guess old habits die hard."

"Well, it's sweet of you to come by. You've always been such a nice person." She glanced over at Ethan. "Just the type of girl I'd like for my son."

His face turned red. "We're just friends, Mom. You know that."

Rebecca's eyes met Ethan's, and she smiled. "My parents used to say the same thing. They don't approve of Pit, but then again, neither do I." She waved her hand. "That's a story for another time." Her gaze moved to Mom. "My parents told me to tell you not to worry about Freddy. They'll keep an eye on him for as long as you need."

My heart sank when I heard my son's name. Although I was truly grateful to my parents for giving him a home when I couldn't, I hated myself for the fact that they had to raise him instead of me.

I'd left him an orphan now, and it was all because of Jeremy. I vowed to make him pay for stealing my life from me. At least he couldn't get to Freddy, and that's what was important.

"Thank you, darling," Mom said, and then turned her attention to Ethan. "Have you been able to reach your sister?"

He shook his head. "No. There's still no answer."

"Your grandmother figured that would happen, so she went up to the Wickcliffs to find her."

"She did? She never goes up there."

"Well, she felt like this time was different. If anyone can find Shelly, she will."

"I hope Gram does. Shelly must've received my messages."

Before Mom could comment, they were interrupted by Rebecca's phone ringing. She opened her purse and took her phone out. She glanced at the caller ID and sighed. "Will you both excuse me for a moment?" She went to the other side of the room.

Ethan and Mom couldn't help but overhear her conversation with Pit as her voice got increasingly louder.

"I told you I was going to the hospital. I'll get home when I get home!"

Pit was Rebecca's deadbeat husband. I'd never liked him, the little I knew about him, and neither had anyone in my family. We never understood why someone like Rebecca married him. The truth was she'd wanted to escape her life at home because her parents were strictly religious, and she had felt trapped growing up.

Rebecca ended the call and returned to them. "Sorry about that."

Ethan smirked. "You two are fighting again, huh? Some things never change. What was it this time?"

"Hell if I know. He sounds agitated for some reason. When the king beckons, he expects me to come running. That's gotten old."

The three of them turned when Dr. Alex Marsh came into the waiting room. He appeared exhausted and ran his hands through his salt and pepper hair.

"Is Jeffrey okay?" Mom asked.

"Just tell us, doctor. Is my dad alive?"

"Your father's alive," Dr. Marsh said, "but there was a complication."

"What do you mean by complication?" Mom held onto Ethan's arm.

"Jeffrey had another attack, and his heart stopped for a few minutes. We were able to get it going again which was a small miracle considering the damage the first attack caused."

Mom put her hand over her mouth and said nothing.

Ethan expected more of a reaction out of her. He wondered if she honestly cared if Dad lived or died. For whatever reason, there was always something in the back of his mind that made him believe that Mom didn't genuinely love Dad. Those old feelings were rising to the surface again.

"Is my dad going to be okay?" he asked.

"I honestly don't know, Ethan," Dr. Marsh said. "At this point, we've done everything we can. The rest is up to him. The next 72 hours are the most critical. It's a good thing you're back in town. Your father may need you."

"Can we see him?"

"I don't see any reason why not. It might do him some good to hear your voices. But remember, he's in critical condition, so I only want one person in there at a time, and you can't stay long."

Ethan nodded.

Dr. Marsh glanced at Mom. "Do you have any questions, Carol?"

"I'm just trying to take it all in, I suppose," she said. "Thank you for telling us."

When Dr. Marsh walked out, Ethan turned to her. "Hopefully the worst is over, huh?"

She gave him a nod and then looked away. There was something my mother was sensing, but she wasn't opening up to anyone.

* * * *

Now that I knew my father was stable, all I could think about was what Mom said about Gram. She was coming to the mansion to find me. She was undoubtedly the most stubborn person I had ever met, and I doubted that she'd leave until she found out my whereabouts. I didn't want her to be the one to find me, though. It probably would be too much for her heart to take.

Along the winding road to the mansion, Gram drove cautiously past Lover's Bluff, her mind drifting into the past. Memories she had thought long forgotten came back to her like water gushing through a burst dam.

She had once worked at the mansion when she was a young woman and thought about those days. She'd started off as a maid, but it didn't take long for her to become mistress to Harold Wickcliff, Jeremy's father.

Back then Gram had been naïve, taken in by Harold's looks and charming demeanor. It wasn't long before his wife, Irma, found out about the affair and banned Gram from the mansion.

Gram had vowed she'd never return and hadn't been back in decades. Tonight she had no choice. She needed to make sure that I knew what was happening to my father.

She pulled up to the gate that led to the mansion. Before she got out of the car, she looked at herself in the rearview mirror. It was dark, but the interior light revealed enough of her reflection, showing her age. Every wrinkle on her face convinced her that she was indeed in her early seventies. She had never thought of herself as old, but time had taken its toll on her.

At times, she barely recognized herself anymore. She now had short curly gray hair and wore glasses. Her face was soft but wrinkled, and her skin had age spots.

For a brief instant, she imagined herself as she'd once looked in the days when she worked at the mansion as a servant. At that time, her hair had been auburn and hit her shoulders softly. Her skin had been plump and vibrant; her brown eyes had shown the glimmer and innocence of youth.

She stopped thinking about the past and got out of the car, approached the small gate and opened it. A creaking sound of rusted metal filled the night air.

She walked up the path that led to the mansion, using only a small flashlight on her keychain to illuminate the dark path. The chirping of crickets surrounded her, and in the distance, she heard the howling of a wild dog or was it a wolf?

Anyone else at her age would've been terrified to walk along this dark path alone at night, but not her. She wasn't the type that was easily frightened, and, at this point, all she cared about was getting me to come to the door so she could tell me what happened to my father. She hoped we could go to the hospital together.

Gram soon found herself at the bottom of the steps that led up to the massive, carved-oak front door. She climbed them and then used the large, metal knocker that was in the shape of a gargoyle. Touching it made her cringe.

She stood there for a minute waiting before hearing footsteps approaching. When the door finally opened, a short, plump woman, stood there wearing a pink robe with curlers in her hair. Gram had never seen her before.

The woman stared and grimaced at Gram. "Well?" She paused. "Are you the one that was banging on the door earlier tonight? I came all the way down here to answer the door, and there was no one. I haven't been able to get back to sleep either I'll have you know. I'm not pleasant when I don't sleep."

"I couldn't imagine," Gram said, raising her eyebrows. "It wasn't me. I just got here. My name's Edith Ford. I'm looking for my granddaughter Shelly."

"I'm Greta, the maid. I've never seen you around here before."

"That's because I don't come up here."

Greta raised an eyebrow. "So you pick now for a visit? Do you have any earthly idea what time it is?"

"I'm sorry, but Shelly's father is in the hospital. He's had a heart attack, and I need to see her right away."

Greta's face softened slightly, but Gram could tell that she was still perturbed.

"Mrs. Wickcliff mentioned something about going out a few hours ago," Greta said. "I don't think she's returned. I'll tell her you were here." She started to shut the door.

Gram put her hand on the door. "Shelly never leaves this house. She's been a recluse for years. Her family hardly sees her, and you're telling me that she's just left?"

"That's right."

Gram stepped forward, blocking the door with her foot, and peered inside. "Even if she did go out, she's got to be back by now."

Greta glared down at Gram's foot and then at her. "Well, I haven't seen her. Please remove your foot."

Gram continued to peer inside. "Maybe Irma knows where she is."

"It's late. The elder Mrs. Wickcliff's asleep and she needs her rest. I told you I'd give your granddaughter the message."

"Greta, you either let me in now, or I come back in an hour with Sheriff Withers. Do you seriously want to be woken up twice tonight?"

Greta sighed heavily and stepped aside letting Gram enter the house.

The house gave Gram the same sick feeling it always had. It had always seemed like more of a mortuary than a home, and it still did. The mansion was cold and lifeless, gray and drab. Once ostentatious, it was now dark and unkempt, just as the outside was. It was hardly warm and inviting as was her family home.

Gram turned her head to Greta. "I want to see Irma."

"You don't understand. She's not well. She's extremely old, and she's ill."

"What do you mean? She can speak, can't she?"

"She gets confused, easily agitated, and short-tempered."

Gram snickered. "I thought you said she wasn't like herself."

"Very amusing, Ms. Ford."

"Sorry, but you just described the Irma I used to know."

"Mrs. Wickcliff's condition isn't humorous. I meant to say that she suffers from dementia."

Gram put her hand on her chest. "Are you serious?"

"Very."

"Well, how the mighty have fallen, how appropriate."

Greta gasped. "Have you no sympathy? That's a terrible thing to say."

Gram exhaled sharply. "Irma had no sympathy for me, Greta. When I worked here, she treated me and the rest of the staff like slaves."

"You worked here?"

"Yes, a long, long time ago, just as you do now. Irma ran the staff ragged from morning to night with not so much as a thank you. One time, she fired a woman for spilling coffee on her uniform, said she didn't care about her appearance."

"I know nothing about that."

"That's right, you don't know. Irma made my life a living hell. Don't talk to me about sympathy."

Gram started for the stairs, but Greta tried to get in the way.

"You don't want to test me right now," Gram said, putting her hand up. "I'm tired, and I'm sore. I ache from head to toe. Do you have any idea what that's like?"

"No, not really."

Gram pushed her to the side with her arm. "You will if you don't get the hell out of the way." She started up the steps. "My granddaughter needs to be with her family right now. If she isn't here, I need to find out where she went. Irma!"

Greta followed right behind her. "If you must insist, I'll take you to Mrs. Wickcliff. I can't have you yelling out her name and wandering around in this house alone."

Gram stopped on the step. "What are you afraid I'll find?"

Greta grimaced. "This is private property, Ms. Ford. How would you like someone poking around your home so late at night?"

Gram didn't answer. Instead, she looked straight ahead and continued to ascend the staircase. As she did, she thought back about Harold. She couldn't believe how quickly the time had passed.

On her way up, she noticed the faded wallpaper that was on the wall halfway up the stairs. It was peeling off. She remembered the day she helped hang it. It had been so crisp and new then. Now it was old and tattered.

Once she and Greta reached Irma's room, Greta opened the door and stepped inside. Greta turned on a light by the bed.

Gram was aghast by Irma's appearance. Irma's hair was sticking up, grayish-white, more like porcupine quills than hair. Her skin was pale and sagged off the bone. Gram was stunned at how emaciated she appeared.

Gram watched as Greta approached Irma and put her hand on the old woman's shoulder softly. "Mrs. Wickcliff? Wake up, dear. You have a visitor."

Irma groaned. "Who is it?"

Gram stepped closer. "It's Edie, Irma. Edie Ford."

"Who?"

"Edith Ford!"

Irma sat up in bed and stared at Gram. "Oh, Edie, I haven't seen you in ages. But must you shout? You'll wake Harold."

Gram raised an eyebrow and glanced over at Greta and then back at Irma. "Irma, Harold's—"

"Remember what I told you," Greta whispered in Gram's ear. "You'll see."

"What did you say to her?" Irma glared at Greta, having heard her say something. "What did you tell Edie? I won't tolerate the help talking about me behind my back in my home. Do you hear me? I'll have you both dismissed." Irma paused and looked at Gram. "Wait a minute, you said you were Edie, but you're not her. You're old."

"Irma, listen to me—" Gram said.

"I told you never to come back to this house. You're nothing but a hussy." She pointed to the door. "Get out or I'll have Jeremy throw you out."

"Jeremy's dead, Irma," Gram said flatly. "So is Harold. Don't you remember anything?"

Irma tugged at her hair, and her eyes lost focus. "Dead? I'm so confused."

Gram raised her chin and then approached the bed. "Irma, I have a granddaughter now. Her name's Shelly. She was married to Rory, remember? She lives here with you."

Irma's eyes brightened. "Ah, yes. Rory and she married. I remember now."

Gram nodded and smiled. "That's right. And she lives here in this house with you. Have you seen her tonight?"

Irma rubbed her temple. "I don't know."

Greta spoke up. "She came up here to see you tonight, Mrs. Wickcliff."

Irma's eyes widened, and she nodded. "Yes. I remember. She said she was going to get my dinner, but she never came back. She looked disturbed as she so often does." She paused and rubbed her stomach. "I'm hungry. What did you say your name was dear?"

Gram exhaled slowly. "Never mind." She turned to Greta and walked away from the bed. "This was a waste of time."

Gram left the room and went into the hall. A moment later, Greta came out of Irma's room, shutting the door behind her.

"I told you she wasn't well," Greta said. "But you wouldn't listen."

Gram waved her hand. "It doesn't matter. Someone blew her pilot light out years ago before she even became senile."

"May I escort you out, Ms. Ford?"

"I know my way around here. I'll let myself out."

Gram realized that she wasn't going to get anything out of Irma, Greta, or anyone else in the Wickcliff mansion tonight. Feeling defeated, she dropped her shoulders and descended the staircase.

Once outside the mansion, she went back to her car, irritated by the encounter with Irma that got her nowhere and worried about me even more.

At her car, she stared up at the mansion. "Where are you, Shelly?"

* * * *

Not long after, Gram arrived back at the hospital and found Ethan and Mom talking.

"Did you speak with Shelly?" Mom asked Gram. "Is she with you?"

"I couldn't find her," Gram said. "The maid said she wasn't there and left the house earlier. I even tried asking that old crone, Irma. She knew nothing. I'm sorry, darling."

Mom rubbed her temple. "Shelly never leaves that house. Where else could she be?"

"I don't know," Gram said, shaking her head. "The maid said she went out. I wasn't about to spend the whole night searching the dark corridors of that place."

"You shouldn't have gone up there alone anyway," Ethan said. "I'll find her. Come on." He motioned to the door. "Let's go see Dad."

Gram's eyes perked. "Is Jeffrey alright?"

"He's stable," Ethan said.

Gram put her hand on her chest. "That's such good news."

"For a minute I thought I was the only one who thought so," Ethan said, shooting Mom a disapproving look.

"He's still in critical condition, Ethan," Mom said, defending herself. "I just don't want to have false hope until I know for sure what's going to happen. Why don't you go see your father first? He hasn't seen you in so long. Maybe it would help his recovery."

Ethan glared at her and then over at Gram. "Fine, I'll be back."

He left the room in a huff, incredulous that our Dad could be dying and that it didn't seem like Mom cared.

* * * *

Outside Dad's room, Ethan stood in the doorway for a moment, almost too afraid to go in. He looked inside and saw wires everywhere. Dad was lying in bed, hooked up to various machines and an IV. He barely saw him there through all the mess including a tube sticking out of Dad's nose. The weak and frail man that lay there didn't even seem like our father to Ethan or me. He remembered how strong, virile and lively Dad had been the last time he saw him.

Ethan took in a deep breath and walked into the room. He pulled out a chair, sat down and took Dad's hand in his.

Dad opened his eyes and groaned. "Shelly, is that you?"

"No, Dad. It's Ethan."

Dad turned his head to face him. "Ethan? I'd hoped you'd come home and here you are."

Unable to control his emotions, Ethan's eyes moistened, and he bowed his head. I wanted desperately to be able to comfort my brother as he had tried to comfort me the last time we spoke.

"Why are you crying, son? Where am I?"

Ethan clutched his hand harder. "You're in the hospital. You had a heart attack, but you're going to be okay now."

"Are you sure?" He paused. "I'm dying, aren't I? That's why you're crying."

"No. You're going to be fine, Dad."

Dad turned his head and stared in front of him blankly. "I remember now. I saw the doctors working on me. I could see my body here lying on the bed." He turned his head to Ethan. "How long do I have to be here?"

Ethan wiped his eyes. "It's gonna take some time for you to heal. Then we'll get you out of here and get you home."

Dad put his free hand on top of Ethan's. "In case I don't make it, I want you to know I love you, and I understand why you left."

"I love you too, Dad. I'm going to stay here and help out with the company until you're on your feet again."

Dad looked beyond Ethan. "Is your mother here?"

Ethan managed a half smile. "Of course she is. And Gram too. They're in the waiting room."

Dad tried to sit up and groaned. "I need to see your mother."

Ethan got up and put his hand on Dad's shoulder. "Don't try to get up. You need to relax. I'll get her. Maybe Shelly's here by now too."

"Oh, God." Dad's eyes widened. "I remember now. I was on my way to see Shelly when I had the heart attack. She's in trouble."

"Is that why you called out for her when you woke up?"

Dad tried to nod. "She called me. She said *he* was coming back."

Ethan cocked his head. "Who was?"

"Jeremy Wickcliff."

Ethan exhaled swiftly. "He's dead, Dad."

"That's not going to stop him from trying to come back to life. The Wickcliffs have powers, Ethan."

Ethan shook his head. "What are you talking about?"

"It sounds crazy. I never talked about it when you two were kids. You were too young to understand. You don't know what happened to us."

"What happened? Why couldn't you tell us?"

"Jeremy died, and we thought it was all over. We wanted to forget everything that happened. The whole town did."

Ethan tilted his head. "Mom knows about this too, doesn't she? When I was a kid, I heard you guys talking about it when you thought I was asleep."

Dad yanked out the IV in his arm. "That doesn't matter now." He tried to get up again. "We have to stop him. I've got to get to Shelly."

Ethan put his hands on our father's shoulders again. "Dad, you need to calm down. Tell me, what does Shelly have to do with this?"

"She was crying, and she wasn't herself. She hasn't been for a long time. She said that she'd been hearing Jeremy's voice. This had been happening for a long time, even before Rory died. Jeremy was telling her she had to die so he could live again. I have to get there before it's too late." Dad tried to push himself up and get out of bed.

"Dad, please." Ethan struggled to restrain him. "You have to lie down."

Dad pushed Ethan's hands away from him. "Let me go. I need to get to your sister." His expression turned grave and then he laid back and groaned with pain. "What if it's too late? What if she's already gone?"

"Gone?"

He looked at Ethan with pain-filled eyes. "What if she's dead?"

Ethan shook his head, and all he could think to do was lie. "Shelly's fine. In fact, she's on her way right now."

Dad's eyes opened wider. "You talked to her?"

"Yeah. She'll be here."

"Thank God." Dad laid his head back on the pillow. "I'll feel better once I see her for myself."

"Don't worry about that right now." Ethan patted his hand gently. "You just need to rest."

"I am tired. I'm glad that someone spotted my car and called for help. I guess I was lucky."

Ethan smiled. "Yes, you were."

Mom came to the door, peeked in and knocked. She saw Dad and smiled at him. "Hey, sleepyhead. You're awake. I know the doctor said one at a time, but I thought maybe you two were finished catching up."

Dad glanced at Ethan. "Go on, son. Your mother and I need to talk."

Mom saw the grave expression on Dad's face. "Are you alright? What's going on?"

"It's about Jeremy Wickcliff," Dad said, not skipping a beat. "He's coming back."

Mom's face hardened, and she turned to Ethan. "You heard your father. I'll catch up with you in a few minutes. Why don't you try your sister again?"

Dad glared at Ethan. "I thought you said you talked to her?"

Ethan put his hand on Mom's shoulder and looked her straight in the eye. "Remember I just told you, Mom? Shelly called, and she'll be here soon."

"Oh," Mom said, nodding. "Of course. With all that's going on, I must've forgotten."

"You're both lying," Dad said, his eyes bouncing back and forth between them. "I can tell." He focused on Ethan again. "You haven't talked to your sister at all, have you?"

"Dad..."

He attempted to get out of bed again. "I can't believe that you'd lie to me, Ethan. I told you Shelly was in trouble, and you almost stopped me from saving her."

He moved his legs out from the bed. Mom went around to the other side of the bed and caught him before he fell to the floor. Ethan rushed to her side to help her with him. They each held him up by one arm.

Dr. Marsh came into the room with a nurse by his side. "What the hell's going on in here? I heard shouting from all the way down the hall."

"I have to get out of here," Dad said as Mom and Ethan tried to get him back in bed. "My little girl's in trouble."

Dr. Marsh and the nurse took over and helped him get back in bed. Ethan and Mom stepped back.

"Take it easy," Dr. Marsh said, helping Dad lay down. "You've been through quite an ordeal. This will only make it worse."

Dr. Marsh turned his attention to Ethan and Mom and scowled. "What did the two of you say to him?"

Dad grabbed the doctor's arm. "I'm wasting time here." He tried to get out of bed again. "I have to go."

"He needs to be sedated," Dr. Marsh said, turning to the nurse. "Now."

With Ethan's help, Dr. Marsh held Dad down until the nurse came back with a syringe and injected it into his arm. The injection made him relax almost immediately.

"Put the IV back in and get the heart monitoring equipment back on," Dr. Marsh said to the nurse. He then turned to Ethan and Mom pointing to the door. "You two need to leave now."

Dad glanced at Mom, his eyes getting heavy. "Promise me you'll protect our family from Jeremy as you did before."

"Just rest," Mom said, touching his hand softly. She moved towards the door. "I'll see you soon."

Ethan followed Mom out having heard what Dad had said to her. When they got into the hallway, he grabbed her arm and led her away from the door. "Will you tell me what the hell's going on? What did Dad mean protect our family as you did before?"

Mom's eyes dropped to the floor, and she shook her head. "It was nothing. He's on a lot of medication, and he's confused."

"That's bull! You know something about Jeremy Wickcliff. Dad said something happened years ago. What was it?"

Mom's face reddened and her eyes rose to meet his. "Jeremy's dead. Do you understand? I'm not going to waste my time talking about a pig like that. There's no point." She started down the hallway. "I need to find your sister."

He called after her, but she didn't turn around. He'd thought he was the only one in his family with secrets, but that was obviously not true. Our parents were keeping events in the past from him that involved Jeremy. Mom tried to convince him that Dad didn't know what he was saying, but he didn't seem so confused. In fact, he seemed quite lucid.

Ethan wondered if Dad was right about me, and if I were in trouble or even dead.

Chapter 8

"Poor Jeffrey," Jeremy said, with a sneer.

I came out of my thoughts, once again in the attic. I turned to find that Jeremy had reappeared in the painting.

"What do you know about my father?"

"Only that his pathetic life's hanging on by a thread. He's only one breath away from death. Oh, how I wish he'd die."

"Well I'm sorry to disappoint you, Jeremy, but my father's going to live and you're not. This sick plan of yours isn't going to work."

Jeremy chuckled. "He's the one that's sick. Sick, weak, vulnerable. You'll be found, he'll die, and your family's going to fall apart. I can't wait to relish in their suffering. No one deserves immense pain and tragedy more than the Hawkins family."

"Why do you hate my family so much? Why do you delight in watching us suffer?"

"It's a story for another time, and frankly, time's almost up. It's time for the final phase of my plan to be implemented at Midnight's Edge."

"You think you're so smug, don't you? You think you know it all and have got it all figured out."

"I do. On both counts. I can see everything you see. You're the one who thinks she's so smug, making contact with the living. That's a beginner's parlor trick. Kasey Menze may hear you, but he can't do anything to stop me. He can't help you. It's too late for you. And what's the point of seeing your useless family? None of them can even hear you, and they don't know that you're there."

"At least when my family finds out what happened, I'll be mourned and missed. Nobody ever mourned you. In fact, nobody in town ever even talked about you. You were hated when you were alive, and now you're forgotten. The only thing you can do is taunt me from that stupid painting. And even that isn't working anymore."

"I wasn't hated, I was feared."

I nodded. "Sure you were. That's what led to the hatred." I paused, exhaling deeply, delighting in the fact that I'd finally found the courage to stand up to him. "I'm not going to be a victim anymore. I'm a spirit now. Now we're equal."

"You'll never be my equal!"

"You know what I think? I think you're afraid. You're afraid that your plan won't work and that you'll be trapped in that painting forever. I can see it in your face."

I could tell that I was getting to him. I knew that if I could keep goading him, I'd get him to tell me everything I needed to know.

"You're wrong as usual."

I put my hands on my hips. "Well, if I'm so wrong, why don't you enlighten me? How did you become as you are?"

He didn't say anything.

"We're both stuck here. We might as well talk to each other."

Jeremy glared at me a moment and then he began. "It all began with my father, Harold. He spent his entire mortal life dedicated to the occult and black magic. He taught me everything I knew in my mortal life and promised me that if I followed in his footsteps I would be rewarded with everything I ever wanted in life and beyond.

"I spent my mortal life being selfish, manipulative, and underhanded, studying the dark arts with my father. I acted the same way in which my father had because it appeared as if it worked for him. During my youth, it seemed as though my father had everything he ever wanted, and I wanted to be just like him.

"However, after I died and entered the ghost realm, I found that the afterlife I was banished to wasn't exactly what my father promised. I soon learned that rather than having everything, I had nothing but my mind. It didn't matter though considering that my intelligence was far superior to anyone else I'd ever encountered. I had an excellent teacher in my father, and I was the ideal student. I learned everything and absorbed everything he told me right down to the last detail.

"I devised a plan to return to the mortal realm using my father's dark powers passed on to me. My first step was to break the barrier and communicate with those in the mortal realm. My father taught me that there were specific steps I had to take in order for that to happen.

"At first I didn't know with whom I'd try to communicate. Then I realized that you would be the perfect victim and that driving you mad would be the ultimate revenge."

My eyes widened. "Revenge for what?"

"Your grandfather, Charles Hawkins, killed my father. I've hated every Hawkins since and want to see nothing more than you all suffer just as you made my family suffer."

I shook my head. "I don't believe you."

He shrugged within the portrait. "Don't believe me? I have nothing more to gain by lying to you. I already got what I wanted when you took your last breath."

My heart sank when I realized that he was right. He had nothing to gain. My parents had kept secrets from me. I began to think my whole life was a lie.

"And you thought you had secrets." Jeremy chuckled. "You weren't the only one with skeletons in your closet. Your whole family is nothing but a lying bunch of hypocrites."

I wanted to scream, but I held back. "So then what?"

"I watched from the ghost realm as you married my cousin, Rory. I believed that a Hawkins married to a Wickcliff shouldn't have been. That's when I decided to destroy your life. Once I decided whom to communicate with, I had to figure out how to do it. I decided to use this portrait of myself as a portal between the different realms. I realized that in order to get you into a state where you'd be susceptible to my urgings, I'd first have to wear you down and try to exhaust you so that you'd have no strength left to resist my demands.

"I did this by going after Rory first. We share the same bloodline, and that made contacting him easier. It was almost as if we were part of one another, a small part of my lineage was in the mortal world. My goal was for Rory to die, and eventually my plan succeeded." He sighed. "In any event, losing Rory blew your world apart, and that was my opening to dispose of you."

Tears of rage began to fill my eyes. "You sick son of a bitch."

Jeremy put his hand up. "Flattery will get you nowhere. I know my plan was genius, but I don't need you to tell me that. You see, once you were depressed and grieving, all you needed was a little push to descend into madness."

I wiped a single tear from my cheek quickly, refusing to let him see that he'd gotten to me again.

"The plan wasn't as easy as I thought," he said, "having taken five mortal years to progress. But, if nothing else, I was persistent.

"I started out communicating with you only in your dreams in the few moments that you did sleep. Slowly, day by day, month by month, I was able to get inside your mind while you were awake. By the end, my voice was all you heard. I finally had control of your mind, and like a slave you listened to everything I said."

"If it weren't for you, Rory would be alive, I'd be alive. We'd still be married."

Jeremy sneered. "I'm not the one that pulled the trigger am I?"

"Pig."

"Shall I continue? I thought so." He paused, giving me a conceited grin. "Once I had control of your every thought and every emotion, it was time for the next phase of my plan, you'd have to die. The death of someone so kind and innocent like you would give me the power I needed to be strong enough to bring my spirit back to the mortal realm in the body of another."

I nodded. "And that's where ME comes in? Where the barrier between the realms is broken?"

"It's my opportunity to live again."

"You did all of this just to get revenge on us?"

"Partly. But regardless of what you Hawkinses think, the universe doesn't revolve around you. I have other reasons to return to the mortal world, and my return is just the beginning. I have to admit that it was fun watching in anticipation as you stepped off that chair, hanging yourself. It couldn't have ended any better for me; the noose wasn't tight enough, and you didn't die right away. You spent the last moments of your life with a crushed windpipe gasping for breath. I was delighted to watch you die slowly."

"I don't remember any of that."

"What a pity."

I held my anger back because I needed to get more from him. "Now what? What's next?"

"Now that you're dead, all I need is someone young and strong to stumble upon my painting, someone like you who isn't strong enough to resist my will. It needs to be a man because I need a strong, virile body."

"I won't let that happen."

He let out a sharp laugh. "And you plan to do what in your current state? Face it, you're helpless at the moment. Once I'm alive again, I can focus on finding my biological son, the one who was taken from me long ago because of my deceitful wife, Lucy, and who was kept hidden from me. I doubt that he's far from Sleepy Meadows, probably been kept by one of her friends. I can sense that he's near. Once I find him, the man who shares my bloodline, I must inhabit him to survive. It must happen this way if I'm to live. Whomever I inhabit first can only be a temporary host until I find my son. Once I find him, the Wickcliffs will rise from the ashes like a phoenix returning from the fire."

The confidence that I had moments ago faded. In the last several moments, I'd found out my family had lied to me, that Jeremy killed my husband and that it was even worse than I thought. Not only one Wickcliff was coming back, but he had a plan to bring back the entire sick and twisted clan. I returned to feeling helpless and hopeless.

"In the meantime," he said, "I'll be entertained with you being trapped here. I'm relishing the fact that it was you who helped me achieve my plan."

"I've heard enough."

"Rory shouldn't have married a Hawkins, and because of that, I made sure I separated you."

I turned away from him and shut him out of my mind. At least I could do that, but where I found my thoughts frightened me even more.

Chapter 9

When I began to think about Rebecca's husband, Pit Bowen, I didn't understand why my thoughts would focus on him particularly after the revelations that Jeremy had just given me.

Why would my thoughts gravitate to him instead of someone in my family or someone else I loved? I barely knew Pit. I'd spent the last several years as a recluse and had rarely seen Rebecca or her husband. As I continued to watch him, though, I got the feeling that I was gravitated to him because it had something to do with my current predicament.

I watched as he went to the fridge, got a beer and then plopped down in his easy chair in front of the TV. When he opened the beer, it spilled all over his white wife-beater t-shirt.

"Son of a bitch!" He stood up quickly and before he could wipe the beer off, his eye caught a glimpse of the mess he'd made earlier when he threw the phone at the wall after Rebecca hung up on him.

He didn't know what he got out of his screwed up marriage and didn't know why he even bothered trying. He downed what was left of the beer, and slammed the empty Bud Light can on the coffee table, belching at the same time.

"Look what that bitch made me do! All she does is disrespect and treat me like an idiot. And it doesn't help that those legs of hers are closed up tighter than Fort Knox." He got up, scratched his belly, and went back to the fridge. "She needs to learn the meaning of respect." He grabbed another beer. "Maybe I'll be the one to teach her one way or another. She's getting too mouthy, too bold. She needs to be knocked down a peg or two."

Pit stopped talking to himself when he heard the kitchen phone ring. He didn't feel like being bothered by anyone tonight and wished that he'd broken that phone too.

He grumbled and decided to answer it when it kept ringing. Maybe it was Rebecca. Maybe she changed her attitude and was coming back home.

The person on the other end wasn't Rebecca, but Gaul, who paid him for odd jobs. Pit was one of the few in Sleepy Meadows who knew that Gaul was much more than what he seemed. He didn't know what Gaul was exactly, but he knew he wasn't human.

"What do you want?" Pit asked. "It's late, and I'm tired."

"Get over here now," Gaul said in his deep, emotionless voice. "I need your help."

"I've been drinkin'. I ain't going anywhere tonight."

"Shelly's killed herself."

I knew it. I knew there was a reason I was seeing Pit now. He was going to become entangled in this mess. Why was Gaul calling him? Had he been the body that Jeremy intended to inhabit at ME once he got to the attic and found Jeremy's portrait? I couldn't think about that now. I had to focus on what they were saying.

Gaul's voice seemed to echo in Pit's ear, sobering him up. "What the hell did you just say?"

"You heard me."

Pit popped open his next beer and took a swig. "What do you want me to do about it? I barely know her."

"I need you to come to the house and help me remove the body before anyone discovers what happened. I can't have a scandal like this befall the family. They've had enough in recent years as it is."

I couldn't believe what I'd heard. Not only did Jeremy force me to take my life, he was going to have the fact that I committed suicide covered up. Would they try to make it look like natural causes? In a way, I was glad. It might spare my family some pain if the truth about the suicide were withheld.

"Just because I've worked for the Wickcliffs doesn't mean that I have to deal with this," Pit said. "You people are nuts. You're on your own."

Gaul's voice rose. "You'll come and bring that young man, Reed. Tell no one else. You'll be paid quite handsomely for your loyalty and cooperation, as always."

Pit chuckled. "No amount of money can make me do what you're asking."

"Mrs. Wickcliff has enough money to last her three lifetimes. Everyone has a price, Mr. Bowen, especially you. Now get over here."

The phone went dead.

Pit hung the phone up and groaned. He scratched his balding head and went to the fridge again. He took out a six pack of beer for the road, knowing that, after tonight, he was going to need them.

"These crazy bitches are going to be the death of me. Now I have to go out in the middle of the night and risk getting caught lugging a body around all because of a complete whack job."

He went to the closet, grabbed his jacket off the coat rack, and quickly wrote a note to Rebecca placing it on the kitchen table. He didn't even know if she'd come home to read it, and right now he couldn't worry about it.

He left the house, agitated, slamming the kitchen door so hard behind him that he thought he broke the glass. He got into his truck and started to drive.

There was one thing Pit knew about the Wickcliffs, or what was left of them: they didn't like scandals. They had too many secrets, some of which Pit was aware of, and he didn't want to know any more. He'd been bound to them for too long as it was.

He tried to calm down in the truck. At least he knew that he would be paid well for his silence, and when that money ran out, he would ask for more. Knowing this little secret about me killing myself wasn't so unlucky after all.

He thought about me being dead and how he had to be the one to clean up the mess. If he hadn't needed the money so much, he wouldn't have had anything to do with the Wickcliffs in the first place.

He opened his phone and dialed.

Reed answered, half asleep. "Pit? Do you know how late it is?"

"We need to talk."

"Not tonight. I was asleep, and I'm tired."

"I don't give a damn. This is an emergency. I'll be there in a few minutes, and you'd better be ready to go."

"Where are we going?"

"I'll explain when I get there. Just be ready."

A few minutes later, Pit pulled up to the small apartment where Reed lived. He got out of the truck and ran up to the door pounding on it. He heard the door unlock and open.

Reed stood there rubbing his eyes. "Are you trying to wake the whole neighborhood? What's the big emergency?"

"I wouldn't need to pound on the door if you were ready like I told you to be."

"Hey, I'm doing you a favor. Give me a break."

Pit grabbed him by both arms and shook him. "Drop the attitude. Shelly Wickcliff hanged herself tonight. I need to go to the mansion and get rid of the body before anyone finds out, and you're coming with me."

Reed's eyes broadened, and he pulled away. "I'm not amused that you woke me up in the middle of the night for some sick joke. Why don't you go back to one of your sleazy dives if you need entertainment instead of using me for a cheap laugh? Freak." He began to close the door.

Pit forced it to open with his arm. "This isn't a prank. This is for real."

Reed studied his face. "You're serious, aren't you?"

Pit grabbed him by the arm and yanked him out of the doorway. "We're wasting time here. Let's go."

* * * *

"Why did you call me?" Reed asked now inside Pit's truck.

"Because you're young, strong, and you mind your own business."

"I'm also the son of the sheriff."

Pit glanced at him, pulled the truck off to the side of the road, and put it in park. He grabbed Reed by the throat, pinning him against the passenger's side door. Reed gasped, fruitlessly trying to break away.

"You listen to me you little punk. You don't tell your old man about this. You don't tell anybody. I don't need anyone asking questions, especially the sheriff. If Gaul finds out we told anyone, we'll both be dead. Got it?"

Unable to speak, Reed nodded. Pit let go of his hold on him. Reed gasped for air, coughed and clutched his throat. He soon caught his breath as Pit began driving again. "I didn't say I'd tell him. I just meant the sheriff's son would be an unlikely person to pick for something like this."

"I don't care what you meant. Just keep your mouth shut and do what you're told."

"Next time you touch me, I'll have your sleazy ass thrown in jail for assault."

Pit laughed. "I don't think I'm the one with the sleazy ass. You don't want everyone in town knowing what you've been doing with Kasey Menze, do you? I don't think your pop would be too proud of that. What would the town think?"

Reed looked away.

"That's right, pansy boy, I know about you and what you are. If you don't do what you're told, everyone else in town will know too."

Reed locked eyes with him. "You're as despicable as they come."

"Shut up. We're almost there."

Reed looked away again shaking his head. "I don't need this. I never agreed to help you cover up a suicide."

Pit reached over and grabbed his arm, making Reed wince with pain. "You think I want to do this? I don't have a choice, and neither do you. Gaul doesn't want anyone to know about this, and he's already told me, and I've told you. Do you know what that means? It means that we either help him, or we die."

Reed yanked his arm away. "I can't believe you've gotten me into this."

"I had no choice. I'm not going to be the only one that goes down if this comes out. The sheriff's son is my security."

Reed rubbed his arm. "Don't ever touch me again."

"Don't give me reason to. Just keep your trap shut and do what I tell you and we'll get along just fine."

Reed took in a deep breath and leaned back in his seat, realizing he had no choice but to do as he was told.

Pit exhaled and drove on. He pulled up to the Wickcliff mansion not long after, turned off his truck and looked over at Reed.

"Get out."

"No way," Reed said. "I'm not going out there alone."

"It's late, no one will see you. I gotta hide this truck somewhere."

"But..."

Pit reached over and unlatched the passenger door. "Get out I said."

Reed got out and barely shut the door behind him before Pit took off. As he turned and glanced upon the large, rusted wrought iron gate that led to the mansion, he had a feeling of foreboding doom. It was as if every fiber of his being was screaming for him to turn and run.

Meanwhile, Pit parked his truck around back and caught up with Reed without him knowing it. He laid his hand on Reed's shoulder, making him jump.

"Christ!" Reed said. "Don't sneak up on me like that."

"Stop being such a baby. I need you to keep it together, Withers. Don't start wigging out on me. And keep your voice down."

"Asshole."

Pit gestured for Reed to follow him. "Let's go."

They walked up the path to the house and found Gaul standing at the front door, a foot taller than the two men, lurking over them, his face emotionless.

"It's about time," Gaul said. "I've been waiting."

"We came as fast as we could," Pit said.

Gaul grabbed Pit's shoulder and tightened his grip. Pit winced, and his knees almost buckled. Reed smiled slightly. He couldn't help but enjoy the sight of Pit cowering to him.

"Do what I say," Gaul said. "Or there will be consequences."

Gaul let go, and turned his body so they could enter. Pit rubbed his bruised shoulder and entered.

Reed slapped him on the arm from behind. "I think I like him."

"Shut up," Pit said.

Gaul shut the door behind them, motioning to the staircase.

"What if someone sees us?" Reed asked. "Ya know, getting rid of the body?"

"No one will see. The house is still, and Mrs. Wickcliff and the servants are asleep." Gaul motioned for them to follow him.

Pit and Reed followed him up the stairs in silence until they got to the third story and the attic steps.

Midnight's Edge, The Secrets of Sleepy Meadows

Reed stopped at the door. "I don't want to go there," he whispered in Pit's ear. "I've got a bad feeling about this."

"Stop being such a pansy and man up," Pit said. "You know too much. You can't back out."

Gaul led them up the short set of stairs and opened the attic door.

Although I could see them, they were mortals and couldn't see me in the spirit realm. They couldn't see how I hung my head in shame as they glanced at my body still hanging from the rafters, feet dangling, eyes bulged, open and lifeless, still filled with panic and fear.

Pit turned around, not wanting to look at me.

Reed was surprised that Pit was bothered. "What's the matter with you? I thought this was no big deal for you?"

"I...I don't want to look at her face."

Reed smirked. "Stop being a pansy and be a man, remember?" He turned Pit around to face my body. "Look what you made us do. If I have to face this, so do you."

"Get the body down and take it down the back staircase," Gaul said. "And hurry up. There isn't any time to waste."

Reed stared at my body. "What'll we do with her?"

"You'll take her to the family mausoleum," Gaul said, turning to walk out the door. "I'll meet you downstairs."

Gaul left the two men alone in the room.

"Let's go," Pit said, moving towards my body. "We'll cut her down. You grab her feet, and I'll cut the noose and support her head."

Pit picked up the chair that I'd stood on and repositioned it near my body. He stood on it, preparing to cut the noose.

Reed grabbed my legs and pushed up. "I wonder why she did it."

"I don't care. We need to do what we're told. That's all."

"What if my dad does find out?"

Pit glared at him. "No one's gonna find out. Got it? Now quit yapping and help me. Hurry up. I don't want to spend any more time in this dungeon than I have to."

Pit supported my head and shoulders while Reed grabbed my legs and lifted. Soon they had my body down and started carrying it across the room.

Reed hit his foot on the side of the chair and lost his footing, tripping and falling back on the floor. My limp body fell to the floor with a thump. I was horrified, unable to believe that my life was over and that it had come to this.

"Jesus. Look what you did, Withers!"

Reed tried to get up, but he hesitated when he thought he heard another voice behind him. He turned around and saw, leaning against the attic wall, the large painting of Jeremy.

As Reed looked at the painting, the next phase of Jeremy's plan had become clear to me. It hadn't been Pit he was going to use, it was Reed. Like he'd told me, he needed someone young and virile. Of course. Why hadn't I thought of Reed before? I wanted to cry out and warn them even though I knew they couldn't hear me.

"Get up," Pit said. "Now!"

Reed couldn't move. He was frozen and couldn't say anything. He continued to stare at the painting, mesmerized, and suddenly an overwhelming feeling of dread overtook me.

"Leave him alone you son of a bitch! I know you can hear me, Jeremy."

Pit kicked Reed's leg with his foot. "Are you deaf? I said get up!"

Reed didn't answer him. He groaned, grabbed the top of his head and covered it with his hands. His body began to convulse violently as if he were having a seizure.

Pit walked around so he could stare at him in the face. He gasped when he saw Reed's red face, eyes bulging out and bloodshot. He leaned over and grabbed Reed by the arms. "What the hell's wrong with you?"

Reed shook uncontrollably. "Leave me alone! I won't listen to you!"

"Let me in," Jeremy said. "Let me live again. Open yourself up to my will, my being. Let my spirit in and make us one!"

Pit, being mortal, couldn't hear him, but I did. I called out, helplessly standing by as I watched it all happen. I wanted to stop it, but I didn't know what to do.

Pit stepped back in horror, knowing that Reed wasn't talking to him. "Who the hell are you talking to?"

Reed put his hands on his head again, tugging on his hair. He looked up again and pressed his hands against his ears. Sweat poured down his face, and the veins on his forehead protruded out. He shrieked and pointed at the painting.

Pit turned and looked at the painting. Blood dripped from Jeremy's face. The blood soon covered the canvas and began dripping onto the floor towards Reed.

Pit yelped and fell back, horrified. He watched as the painting's canvas bulged out with the frame staying in place. Jeremy's image, now black, started to take on a lifelike form, and pulled itself out of the canvas moving toward Reed.

Pit watched as the black form surrounded and engulfed Reed, vanishing inside him. Reed's body jerked violently, then he choked and convulsed once more. For a brief moment, Reed was still. Then he tried to stand up but fell to the floor again.

Pit held his breath and didn't move, stunned by everything he just saw.

Reed stood up slowly this time and got his footing. A malicious grin formed on his face, and he clasped his hands together.

"No," I said, glaring at him and knowing that it was no longer Reed. "It's you. Damn you!"

Jeremy laughed maniacally. He touched his arms, his face, and legs as if he didn't believe he was there.

"Midnight's Edge," Jeremy said, grinning widely. "It worked. My father was right. It worked. I'm alive again."

Then he glanced at my body on the floor, smiling devilishly. I realized that he could see me no more. I was now alone.

Pit backed up more. "What's the hell's the matter with you, Reed?"

He said nothing, paying no attention to Pit at first. He scanned the room, getting his bearings. He smiled again and let out another devious cackle.

Then he whipped his head towards Pit, and a foul expression washed over his face. His glare was piercing, like the eyes of a shark.

"You're not Reed," Pit said. "Who the hell are you?"

"Reed isn't here anymore. My name's Jeremy Wickcliff."

Pit shook his head. "That's impossible. You need help."

Jeremy raised an eyebrow. "That's right, I do. And it's you that will help me."

Pit shook his head. "You won't get any help from me."

Jeremy moved closer to him, staring into his eyes. "You'll be my slave and do what I tell you, or you'll die. The choice is yours."

Pit laughed. "I'm nobody's slave."

Jeremy glared at him, grabbed his throat, and, with immense strength, pushed Pit up against the far wall. "You'll do what I tell you or else!"

Pit clawed at Jeremy's hands frantically, trying to loosen his grip. Eventually, Jeremy let go, and Pit fell to the floor, gasping for air.

"Do you believe me now? Would Reed Withers have that sort of strength?"

All Pit could do was nod and rub his neck.

"I'm free, and I'm alive." Jeremy glanced towards my direction, although he couldn't see me. He wore an obnoxious, conceited grin. He knew I was looking at him. "And it's all thanks to that bitch. Do you hear me, Shelly? I'm alive because of you."

He pointed towards my body still lying on the floor and turned his head towards Pit. "Now you'll help me move her. We don't have any time to waste."

Chapter 10

I didn't know what to do after seeing Jeremy possess Reed, so I turned my attention back to Kasey, who lied unconscious in the back of the mansion. He had to wake up. I had to try to make contact with him again knowing that he was the only one who could hear me. He began to stir; a moment later, he was awake.

He seemed dazed at first, but after a moment, he got to his feet, suddenly remembering the vision I'd shown him earlier. He'd learned over the years to trust his visions, and he was positive that I was dead. Tears welled up in his eyes, and he grieved for me. His tears also came because he knew he would have to tell Ethan what he'd seen. He didn't want to shatter my brother's heart.

Then he thought there was the distinct possibility that Ethan wouldn't believe him at all and think he'd gone mad. After all, he didn't have absolute proof that I were dead. He couldn't think about the consequences of his vision right now. Ethan and my family needed to know what he saw.

He made his way to the front side of the mansion near the Wickcliff cemetery. He approached the gate slowly, hearing two men's voices in the distance. They were behind him, coming from where he had been standing moments before. He wasn't expecting anyone else to be lurking around at this hour and wasn't sure how he'd explain his presence here if he were caught.

He quickly hid behind a large, gnarly pecan tree near the gates as the voices of the men got closer. He stepped on a small twig, which snapped beneath his foot. The sound seemed to cut the silence that surrounded him. He swallowed and held his breath, hoping that they hadn't heard him.

Pit heard. "What was that sound?"

"Nothing," Jeremy said with annoyance in his voice. "Keep moving. We don't have time to stand around."

Kasey was surprised to hear Pit and Reed's voices. He hadn't known that the two men knew each other that well. Why would they be headed towards a cemetery in the middle of the night? And why was Reed giving Pit orders? It didn't sound like the Reed he knew.

When he heard them walking away, he peered out from behind the tree. He saw them carrying something large and bulky wrapped in a black bag, the size of a body. It appeared as though they were carrying it to the family mausoleum in the middle of the cemetery. He couldn't be sure, though. The fog that began to roll in had obstructed his view. There was also a taller man with them who didn't speak. He hadn't realized it was Gaul.

He got a sick, aching feeling in the pit of his stomach. He wondered if it were me that they were carrying. Maybe they'd found out what I'd done and were taking my body away. Why were they trying to hide it? Why didn't they call the police? Why would Reed be involved?

This time tears of rage welled up in his eyes. He couldn't believe that I was being lugged around like an old piece of furniture that didn't matter at all. I could feel his rage building. It took every ounce of strength he had not to confront them.

Once the men were out of sight, Kasey ran to his bike, which he'd hidden in the bushes nearby and drove away. As he sped past Lover's Bluff, thoughts of me and Ethan consumed him.

He realized he had to do more than just talk to Ethan. It was one thing to explain that he thought that I was dead, but now it appeared as if Reed and Pit were trying to cover it up.

He needed to go to the police and talk to Reed's dad, Graham Withers, the sheriff. He had to tell Graham what he thought his son was involved in.

* * * *

Meanwhile, I had to know what Jeremy was up to. I watched as Pit helped carry my body with Jeremy and Gaul through the Wickcliff cemetery until they reached the mausoleum.

Midnight's Edge, The Secrets of Sleepy Meadows

"We'll put her in here," Jeremy said, as Gaul opened the large steel door.

The door opened with a loud creak. Gaul flipped the light switch.

Once inside, Jeremy pointed to a large stone tomb set near the middle of the gray room. "Put her there," he said to Pit, gesturing with a nod to the tomb. "We'll lie her down."

Pit noticed the inscription on the tomb, which read: 'Rachel Wickcliff'.

Pit recognized the name knowing that Rachel was Jeremy's deceased sister, Irma's only daughter. He'd never met her, only heard stories of her when he was growing up in Sleepy Meadows.

Pit groaned as he lifted my body up onto the tomb.

"Faster," Jeremy said.

Pit groaned. "Give me a break. She's heavier than she looks."

Jeremy smirked and stared at my body. "Shelly was a crazy bitch. I just assumed her diet consisted of Vodka and Prozac. She should be as light as a feather."

Pit laid me flat on the tomb and lowered his head. He was beginning to feel the emotional weight of the situation. At first, all he thought about was how he could use my death to his advantage. He had wondered how much money he could extort from old Irma. Now after seeing me hanging there in the attic and carrying my body out to the cemetery, he was beginning to feel sorry for me.

"Why do you have to talk about her like that, huh?" he said. "She had problems, but she was still a human being."

Jeremy clasped his hands together. "Touching. If I had a heart, it would probably be breaking. You have two choices, Mr. Bowen. You either stop your sniveling and man-up, or you can join your bosom buddy here. What would you prefer?"

Pit glared at Jeremy with both fear and disgust. Then he glanced down at my body again and sighed. "Are you going to leave her laying here like this? I got drug out here in the middle of the night to cover up her death only to leave her here laying out in the open? It doesn't make sense."

It hadn't made sense to me either. What was Jeremy going to do with my body? At first, I had thought that he was just trying to cover up the suicide itself. Now he was hiding my body as if he were trying to cover up my death altogether. My family would come looking for me. Jeremy had to have known that he couldn't cover this up.

"No one ever comes here," Jeremy said. "They don't have reason to. I have plans for the body. Whether it makes sense to you, is none of my concern."

"What if people ask about her?" Pit asked. "What if they think we killed her?"

Jeremy ignored his question, and his eyes shifted to Gaul, who stood there silently. "Ignore this sniveling idiot. You know what to do."

Gaul gave him a nod and pulled a small jar from his pocket. He lowered my nightgown from my shoulders and neck and then put what appeared to be petroleum jelly on both.

Jeremy turned back to Pit. "No one will think we killed her. No one will even know she's dead. You'll see."

I wondered how that would be possible. I had known that Jeremy was devious and cruel, but now I just thought he was crazy.

"The Hawkins family will come looking for her," Pit said. "They're gonna wonder where Shelly is—"

"It's no concern of yours," Jeremy snapped. "I'll handle the Hawkins family." He paused. "Doesn't this Reed character work for them?"

Pit nodded.

"Fantastic. I'll go to the hospital to see Jeffrey and play the concerned family friend and employee. I'll tell them Shelly left for a few days. That she had to get away. I'm sure I can convince them that everything's okay and then continue with my plans."

Pit's eyes widened. "What plans?"

Jeremy pointed to the door. "I told you, they're none of your concern. You're irritating me with all your questions. You can go home now."

"But—"

"I said go before I change my mind and kill you right here!"

Pit moved towards the door.

"Mr. Bowen?" Jeremy wore a smirk on his face. Pit turned back around when he heard Jeremy call him. "This may go without saying, but

I'm sure that I have to spell things out for a simpleton like you. If you tell anyone what happened here tonight or if you tell anyone who I am, you're dead. And don't go too far. I may need your services again, and you'd better make yourself available to me if you want to keep breathing."

Pit tried to swallow, but he had a lump in his throat. He stood there unable to say anything.

"Ugh, you make me sick." Jeremy waved his hand and turned his head. "Get out of my sight."

Once Pit had left the mausoleum, Jeremy noticed Gaul standing over my body. He looked as if he were almost in a trance.

"She's beautiful, isn't she?" Jeremy said, amused by Gaul's reaction. "Although I despised her, I can't deny her beauty."

"I don't remember what it's like to be attracted to a woman," Gaul said. "I lost that emotion long ago."

Jeremy touched his shoulder. "I suppose you would have after what my ancestors did to you. They took everything away from you."

"Not Rachel. She was always my friend."

Jeremy almost felt sorry for him. "You took care of her, and she loved you for that devotion."

Gaul didn't acknowledge what he said.

Jeremy glanced at me again. "Shelly's body will do quite nicely as a host for my sister."

I was horrified at what I'd just heard. Jeremy planned to possess my body with the spirit of his dead sister just as he'd done with Reed and his own. I gave up my life for him and his twisted family, and that sickened me more now than it had before.

He bent down closer to my body. Gaul watched him, devoid of any outward emotion. Although he was not supposed to, feelings inside Gaul were beginning to emerge. Although he was supposed to be without emotion, he'd loved Rachel once, and those feelings were starting to resurface.

I watched Jeremy lay his hand on top of my head and close his eyes. "Hear me dark ones! The elements will not touch this body. With all the power of the Wickcliffs, it's my vow that this body remain perfectly preserved until it's time for my sister to live again."

While there hadn't been rain before, the thunder outside rumbled, and the wind howled.

"We'll start the ritual tomorrow after I return from the hospital," Jeremy said. "I can't wait to pull the rug out from underneath the Hawkins' lives."

Gaul stayed behind when Jeremy left the mausoleum. He glanced down at me with his black eyes and touched the letters inscribed on the tomb with his thick fingers speaking in a soft tone: "My dearest Rachel."

Chapter 11

I had to get through to Kasey somehow now that I knew that the next phase of Jeremy's plan involved bringing his sister back from the dead. Maybe if I could warn him, he could stop Jeremy, but how? I hadn't fully understood my powers yet. The last time I tried to make contact with Kasey, he passed out. How could I do it without scaring him or putting him in physical danger? Would he even be receptive to my attempts after his horrible reaction to the last vision?

As I concentrated on Kasey, I saw the Sleepy Meadows Police Department building come into focus. He'd thought about going to the police after leaving the Wickcliff grounds, and it became apparent to me that he was planning to do just that.

I hadn't seen Kasey pull up on his bike. Instead, my focus was diverted to inside, and I watched as Graham Withers signed some documents at his desk.

He wasn't the typical small-town sheriff. He was a trim, good-looking man in his early 40's whom everyone thought looked younger than his years. It was hard to believe that he had a son in his twenties.

He'd married young and had become a widower after his wife, Sharon, died. People used to say that he reminded them of 'Andy Taylor' from the "Andy Griffith Show" because they were so similar: kind, noble and upstanding, understanding, sympathetic, but not a pushover when it came to upholding the law.

He yawned and glanced at the clock, convinced that it wasn't moving at all. This was a night that was never going to end. Just as he was about to doze off at his desk, he heard the door to the station burst open from his office, which made him jump up.

"I have to talk to the sheriff right now," Kasey said to Raymond, the deputy, at the front desk. "It's an emergency."

Raymond stood up. "What's this about, Kasey?"

"I don't have time to explain that. Just get me the sheriff."

Graham opened his door and peered out into the waiting area at Kasey. He thought Kasey looked pale, his eyes wide with panic. "Kasey, what are you doing here? Do you know how late it is? What the hell's going on?"

"I had to see you. This can't wait."

Graham waved him in and stepped aside allowing him to enter his office. He motioned to a chair across from his desk so Kasey could sit down.

He shut his door and walked to his desk, sat down and leaned back in his chair. "Tell me what's gotten you so upset."

Kasey took in a deep breath and let it out slowly. "I just came from the Wickcliff's—"

"How many times do I have to tell you kids to stay away from there? Do you know how many people I've caught trespassing up there? It's against the law you know."

"I'm not a kid, Sheriff. I didn't go up there for childish pranks." Kasey shook his head. "You don't understand. I was up there for a reason." He sighed. "Do you want to hear this or not?"

Graham sat back. "Okay. I'm sorry. I'm listening."

"I went up there to find Shelly. Her father had a heart attack and no one from the family has been able to reach her by phone."

"I know about Jeffrey. He's a decent man, and I hope he'll be okay." He paused. "Why would you go up there to tell her instead of one of her family members?"

Kasey paused for a moment, thinking about the vision of seeing me hanging in the attic. "It doesn't matter why I did it. The point is I did, and I saw something that disturbed me. I don't think you're going to like it."

Graham leaned forward.

"Reed was up there with Pit Bowen."

Graham's brow furrowed. "What was he doing there? He told me he'd been doing odd jobs, landscaping and such, but in the middle of the night?" He groaned. "What's he doing hanging out with a slime like Bowen? That doesn't even make sense."

"That's not all. I saw them carrying something into the mausoleum on the cemetery grounds, lugging it actually."

Graham ran his hand through his hair. "Just tell me, Kasey. What are you getting at?"

"I think the reason they can't find Shelly..." Kasey shifted his eyes away, looking down at the floor, "is because she's dead."

Graham stood up from the desk and put his hands on his hips. "Why would you say such an outlandish thing? She's been unreachable for a few hours. That doesn't mean she's dead."

Kasey looked straight at him. "Sheriff, if I weren't so sure, I wouldn't be here. I think it was her body that they were lugging."

"How can you be so sure? It's dark and foggy out there. It could've been anything."

Kasey shook his head. "Come on. Think about it. Why else would they be out there in the middle of the night? I know what I saw, but I can't tell you how I know."

"Then I can't help you."

Kasey stood up. "Please, Sheriff, you know me. You know I wouldn't make something up like this."

"I do know you. I know that you've had a drinking problem in the past. You still work at the bar. Have you been drinking again?"

"No. I swear I'm telling you the truth. If I tried to explain it to you, you wouldn't believe me."

"I do believe you, Kasey. I believe that you believe what you saw. Unless someone reports Shelly missing there's nothing I can do, and someone can't even report her missing for 48 hours."

"I'm just as worried about Shelly as her family is. She's like a sister to me." He exhaled. "You probably don't know, but Ethan's back."

Graham raised a brow. "He's back? I haven't seen him since Rory died. No one has."

"I need to know what to tell him. If you doubt what I'm telling you, go up there and check on her. Prove me wrong. I hope to God you can."

Graham didn't know what Kasey saw, but he could tell that Kasey was genuinely shook up. He thought of Kasey as a well natured, decent young man, and knew that he wouldn't come to the police if he didn't genuinely feel there was a need. There was a time when Kasey had problems, but that was a long time ago.

"I'll make you a deal," Graham said. "I'll go up there in the morning if you promise me you'll go home and get some sleep."

Kasey shook his head adamantly. "No. It has to be tonight."

"You're really afraid, aren't you?"

Kasey nodded.

"Alright, I'll go there now. Hopefully the servants don't think I've lost it, poking around the grounds at this time of night." He pointed to Kasey. "You, on the other hand, need to go home now."

"But—"

"Do what I say."

"Okay, thank you, Sheriff."

Graham led Kasey out of the station and then went back to his desk and sat for a few minutes. He leaned back in his chair and rubbed his chin, thinking about what Kasey had told him.

He wondered why Reed was on the Wickcliff grounds at this late hour and why he was hanging out with a lowlife like Pit Bowen. He thought about me and the fear he saw in Kasey's eyes when he told Graham about my death. Graham almost believed him and wished he hadn't.

He stood up abruptly and walked out of his office toward Raymond, who had fallen asleep at his desk. He kicked the deputy's chair.

Raymond sat right up and blinked. "Huh? What? What's up, Sheriff?"

"I need you to hold down the fort." He grabbed his coat, hat and keys near the door. "I'm leaving for a bit."

"Where ya going this late?"

"The Wickcliffs."

Raymond's right eyebrow arched. "Why are you going up there now? It's creepy even in the daylight."

Graham smirked, reached for the door and opened it. "I just need to check something out."

"Are you alright? You seem…concerned."

"I'm fine, or at least I will be. Can I count on you?"

Raymond nodded. "I'll hold down the fort here."

"No more sleepin' on the job." Graham gave him a wink, and then headed out the door.

As I watched him leave, I wondered what the sheriff would find when he arrived at the house. Would he discover the truth about Jeremy? Would he be able to stop him from his plan to bring his sister back from the dead? I wanted to hope so, but I was still too afraid that no one would believe Kasey.

Chapter 12

I wanted to make contact with Kasey, to warn him that Jeremy was back, but I'd seen him pass out earlier in the night after the last vision I'd given him and saw how frazzled he was at the police station. I figured that I could wait a little while and give Kasey a chance to rest. Jeremy said he wasn't planning on starting the ritual to bring Rachel back until the next day. I had time.

I decided to focus my attention on Graham instead. I needed to find out what was going on downstairs and who else knew about what happened to me. I thought maybe Graham could find out something. I watched him in his car as he drove from the station to the mansion.

Graham hated to admit it, but Kasey's visit to the station concerned him. He didn't want to let on because Kasey already seemed on edge, but the urgency in Kasey's voice led Graham to believe that whatever Kasey had seen, or whatever it was he thought he had seen, should be investigated.

Graham's opinion of Kasey was that he was normally a level-headed guy, a person who didn't scare easily, which meant that he couldn't deny that something had obviously freaked Kasey out tonight.

The fact that Kasey had reported seeing something strange up at the Wickcliffs made Graham think about his childhood and his father, Richard, who was also once the sheriff.

He remembered the look of fear on the adults' faces whenever the Wickcliffs were mentioned. He recalled vaguely at one point when his father had imposed a curfew that said that no residents were allowed to leave their homes after dark. Whenever anyone had asked his father about the curfew, he would get agitated and change the subject. Once people realized they wouldn't get answers, they stopped asking.

But for the last fifteen years, besides the shocking death of Rory, everything had been pretty calm, both in town and at the Wickcliff's. Graham wanted to keep it that way.

He kept replaying what Kasey had told him over and over in his mind. He worried about Reed hanging out with Pit Bowen, but he'd have to deal with that later. His main concern was locating me.

Although it was common knowledge that I'd become a recluse, he thought it was strange that I didn't show up at the hospital when my father was admitted or that I hadn't answered any of the phone calls from my family that Kasey had told him about.

Given the hour and the fact that Irma's staff probably wouldn't let him into the mansion to talk to me without one, he woke Judge Banfield out of a sound sleep in order to secure a search warrant.

Banfield was none too pleased to be awakened in the middle of the night, but Graham promised he would explain everything in the morning. He just hoped he could explain.

When he arrived at the mansion, it took a few minutes for Greta to come to the door. If looks could kill, Graham would've dropped over right there.

"Now what?" Greta's expression turned sour. "First I hear someone poking around out here, then Ms. Ford shows up and now you. Don't any of you people sleep?"

"I'm sorry for the inconvenience, Greta, but I need to talk to Shelly. Her father had a heart attack, and she needs to know."

"Ms. Ford, her grandmother, was here earlier. I know about her father's heart attack, but she isn't here. I don't know what to tell you. She went out earlier this evening and hasn't returned."

"Well, how do you know she hasn't returned by now? It's pretty late. She could be back by now, couldn't she?"

"I suppose so."

"I'd like to check her room to see if she's back yet. Strange though, isn't it, that she's gone even though she supposedly never leaves this house?"

Greta shrugged.

"I'd like to go there now. May I come in?"

"You can't just come prowling around here in the middle of the night, Sheriff."

He flashed the warrant to her. "I was hoping to not to have to use this, but I figured you'd say that."

Greta's eyes widened. "A search warrant? Why do you need a warrant? What have we done?"

"It's just a precaution, Greta. Now step aside, please."

Greta moved to the side, and Graham entered the house. She closed the door and turned to face him. "I'll take you up there, but you must be quiet so as not to disturb Mrs. Wickcliff."

Greta led him upstairs to my room. He found my bed not slept in.

"Looks like she never came home," he said. "Did she tell you where she was going this evening?"

"No."

He checked the closets and drawers. All of my clothes were still there. On top of my dresser was my purse. Inside were my credit cards and a few thousand dollars cash.

He held them up. "Couldn't get too far without these. When did you last see her again?"

"Earlier this evening. I told you that already. She mentioned something about coming upstairs to see Mrs. Wickcliff and then she was planning to go out."

"Maybe Irma can tell me what happened."

Greta moved in front of him. "Absolutely not! It's late, and the poor thing is old and confused. I won't have her disturbed again. Ms. Ford already upset her enough tonight."

"Edith talked to Irma? Did Irma tell her anything?"

"She doesn't know what she's saying, Sheriff."

He sighed. "I'll be the judge of that. I promise not to upset her, alright? Besides, you aren't in a position to object. I have a court order allowing me to search this house as I see fit. That includes speaking to anyone I deem necessary."

Reluctantly, Greta took him to Irma's room. They stood outside. Greta put her hand on the doorknob and turned her head to him. "If you insist on talking to her, I can't stop you. She'll probably be just as confused as she always is. Her moments of lucidity are few and far between these days. This is a waste of time."

He nodded. "Point taken, but we're going to try it anyway."

They went inside, and Greta turned on the lamp by the bed. Irma heard them and sat up in bed; her hair stood straight up in the air and almost made Graham laugh.

"Is that you Harold?" she said, squinting her eyes. "I'm not in the mood for any frisky business tonight. I'm tired and cranky. Go back to your room."

Irma plopped her head down on the pillow.

He looked at Greta and then back at Irma. "It's Sheriff Withers, Mrs. Wickcliff. I'm sorry to disturb you, but I need to ask you a few questions."

"I've had enough disturbances for one night, Richard. First Edith Ford and now you. I'm an old woman. Why can't you all just leave me alone?"

He scratched his head. "I'm Graham, Mrs. Wickcliff. Richard was my father."

"Graham? But he's just a little boy. Richard's the sheriff."

"He was at one time, but my father passed away several years ago. You know that."

Irma gasped. "I knew no such thing. When did that happen?"

He tried to change the subject. "Mrs. Wickcliff, you said Ms. Ford was here. Was she looking for Shelly?"

"Shelly who?" Irma said, her eyes dazed.

Greta piped up in the background. "Yes, she was Sheriff. But she wasn't here, and she still isn't. Can we please go now?"

He didn't answer her. "One more question, Mrs. Wickcliff. Did Shelly tell you where she was going?"

For the first time since he walked into the room, Graham saw a look of clarity in Irma's eyes.

"The child was disturbed, you know," Irma said. "She was crying earlier. She said she heard voices."

He stooped down to her level. "Voices? What did they say to her? Did she tell you?"

Irma put her hands on each side of her head. "I don't know. I'm so confused."

Greta came behind him and touched his arm. "I think you'd better leave, Sheriff. She can't take much more of this."

"Richard, you may want to ask Harold. He might know where Shelly went."

Graham straightened his back and realized that Irma calling me disturbed was the pot calling the kettle black.

"What year is it, Mrs. Wickcliff?" he asked.

She told him a date, but she was off by several decades.

He realized that Greta was right. Due to her senility and advanced age, he couldn't bank on anything that Irma said.

After they left the room and had gotten down to the foyer, he turned to Greta. "I have one last question. Have you seen my son, Reed, or Pit Bowen here on the grounds tonight?"

She shook her head. "No. Why?"

He studied her stoic face. He couldn't tell if she was lying or not. "I was told that Reed and Pit were on the property."

"Oh?" Greta put her index finger below her chin. "That's right. I didn't see them, but Gaul told me they were doing some yard work, and they were finishing up. I had forgotten about that."

"Where's Gaul now?"

"He's retired for the night. Would you like me to wake him?"

Graham thought about it. "No, that's okay." He followed Greta to the front door, and she opened the door for him. "Let me know if you see Shelly."

She gave him a nod. "I will, Sheriff."

Graham walked out of the mansion. Before he left, he searched the garage. My car was gone, and that sent up a red flag for him. He wondered why my car would be gone, but my purse with my driver's license and all my money would still be in my room.

After he had walked out of the garage, Graham scanned the property. His eyes stopped on the Wickcliff cemetery, and he started walking towards the gate, thinking about what Kasey had told him about Pit and Reed being there. He noticed how dark it was in the cemetery even with the moonlight breaking through the fog.

He approached the gate and reached out his hand to open it. An overwhelming feeling of dread overcame him, and he lost his breath. He stepped back and began to sweat profusely; his chest tightened.

The wind began to howl, and a gust knocked him back further away from the gate. He looked up into the sky and saw dark clouds forming above him, obscuring the moon. It looked as if it were about to storm any moment.

Then he heard a voice, low and ominous. It commanded him to step backward and leave. The voice went away as quickly as it came. He touched the top of his head, which felt hot. He wondered what was happening to him. His hair was wet, and he felt dizzy. He thought that he must be imagining things.

His phone rang, startling him. It was a call from Raymond at the station. "Sheriff, I need you over here right away. Bart Stoll got drunk and is causing trouble again."

"Okay, I'll be right there."

He put the phone away and glanced through the gate of the cemetery once again. He didn't see anything or anyone. He assumed that I must be with my family at this point, but it was too late to bother anyone else. My family had been through enough with my father's heart attack.

He decided he would check it out in the morning, stop by the hospital and ask my family if I'd been there. Once he dealt with me, he'd turn his attention to why Reed had been here.

Jeremy, Gaul, and Pit thought they had gotten away with covering up my death, but they hadn't banked on the sheriff searching my room. Sheriff Withers wasn't stupid. He was going to realize that something was wrong, and when he did, the whole truth about my horrifying ordeal was going to come out.

Chapter 13

Alone in the attic, I began to feel hopeless again. Graham's visit to the mansion and his suspicion about my car being gone while my purse was still there was something, but it didn't prove that I was dead, and he didn't know anything about Jeremy's return or plan to bring Rachel back to life.

My only hope was Kasey. I'd gotten through to him, but could I depend on him to tell people what he saw in the vision I showed him? He tried to tell the sheriff, and I appreciated that, but would he be able to tell people he saw me dead in his mind without people thinking he'd gone mad? He was worried that people would think he had, and I didn't blame him.

As I stood there, I thought about how I'd thrown my life away, about how I'd left my son without a mother and parents without a daughter. I'd left my brother without a sister. I'd done it to get rid of Jeremy's cruel, taunting voice. I'd thought that I'd have peace and that maybe I'd go to heaven. I didn't expect to be stuck here in the place of my death. I didn't expect to be alone.

I still wasn't strong enough to get out of the attic. I tried the doors and the windows again, but my hand passed right through them. When I touched the wall, my hand went through it, but I was unable to pass through the wall to get to the other side. It was as if there was some force that was preventing me from leaving.

My mind was free to wander the mortal realm, but my spirit body was still trapped in the spirit realm. I had come to the conclusion that being here was my punishment for taking my life. I would be stuck here for eternity alone.

I wondered how Jeremy could have so much power to make me do what I'd done. Then I had a thought. If he could return to the mortal

Midnight's Edge, The Secrets of Sleepy Meadows

realm, maybe I could too. Maybe if I could find a way to get back to my body before he used it for his plan, maybe I could get back to my life and my son. He'd returned during Midnight's Edge, and although I didn't fully understand what that meant, I needed to find out.

With renewed vigor, I searched the attic for a way out. As I searched, I heard what sounded like a faint whisper. Being that I was so desperate for company, I shrugged the sound off, thinking that my mind was playing tricks on me. The voice got louder and clearer as time went on, and I no longer could ignore it.

"Help me. Please, help me."

It was a man's voice, and it wasn't in my head. I started looking around the room for the source. "Where are you? I can't see you."

"I'm here in the painting. I can see you."

I gazed at the painting of Jeremy leaning against the wall. As I approached it, the portrait faded to black. I backed away, afraid that something horrible would appear.

"Don't walk away," the man said. "You have to help me get out."

"I'm not going to fall for any more of your tricks, Jeremy. I've suffered enough thanks to you."

"I'm not Jeremy. I'm trapped inside the painting. I can't get out, and I can't remember how I got here. Please, I'm scared."

I approached the painting cautiously again, knelt down in front of it and reached my hand out.

"You'll have to reach inside and grab my hand. Please hurry. I'm afraid if I don't get out now, I never will. I don't understand any of this, and I need help. I'm begging you."

I was apprehensive. Trying to shake off any doubt, I reached in and slowly put my hand through the canvas.

The man inside the canvas grabbed my hand forcefully. I pulled back, but his grip was firm. "Please don't let go. I'm not going to hurt you."

"I've got you," I said. "Now what?"

"Pull me through!"

I put my other arm inside and felt him grab it. I gritted my teeth, leaned back and pulled him through the canvas inch by inch.

Once his torso was outside the canvas, he reached out, put his hands on the floor and pulled himself out the rest of the way. He collapsed on the floor gasping for breath.

I saw his beet red face, sweat dripping down his forehead. I recognized him immediately. "Reed? How did you get in there?"

Reed's eyes were wide with panic. "I told you I don't remember. I...wait a minute." He backed up. "I remember something. You're dead, stay away from me!"

I put up my hand. "Don't be afraid of me. I'm not going to hurt you. I think if you can see me, maybe you're dead too."

"That isn't true!" He tried to get up but stumbled. "Don't say that! I can't be dead!"

"It's going to be okay, Reed."

His face reddened even more. "How can you say that?"

"I have to believe that and so do you for both our sakes."

"It can't be you, Shelly. I saw your body hanging." He pointed to where my body had been. "Right there."

"It's me. I'm a spirit now, and maybe you are too." I paused for a moment, recollecting what I'd seen earlier. "I know how you got in there. I saw the whole thing. Jeremy inhabited your body. You must've switched places. He took yours, and you took his within the painting."

"That's crazy," he said, pointing to me. "You're crazy. The whole town knows that. There's no such thing as possession."

"Then how can you explain being trapped in that painting?"

He turned to face the canvas that was now empty and then looked back at me. "I can't."

Seeing how upset he was, I put my hand on his shoulder. I was able to touch him, which made me feel connected to something again.

He looked at me with red, swollen eyes, softer and kinder than before. "Why did you do it?"

I balled my fists. "Jeremy made me do it."

"Jeremy? Wait a minute..." He stared off into the distance, remembering.

"Do you remember now?"

"I was up here in the attic with Pit. We were moving your body, and then...I saw the painting. I heard a voice of a man. He told me to let go,

Midnight's Edge, The Secrets of Sleepy Meadows

to let him in. I tried to fight him but…" He looked straight at me. "It must have been Jeremy."

"What else do you remember?"

"Nothing." He groaned. "God! It has to be true. Jeremy stole my life and my body." He looked around the room. "Why do you think we're here?"

"I don't know."

"What is this place?"

"All I know is it's been like hell to me."

His eyes narrowed. "Why do you say that?"

"I can't get out of this place. It's like some horrible trick's been played on us."

"There has to be a way out." He scratched his head. "I need to get out of here."

"Jeremy took our lives in this place. That could mean we're trapped. I wish I had some answers."

He walked past me. "You may be dead, but I'm not. I didn't kill myself. I didn't die of natural causes. Jeremy took my body from me. Do you hear me? I'm not going to accept that I'm dead. I have a life, and I'm going to get it back!" He tried to open the door, but he couldn't grasp it.

I put my hand on his shoulder tenderly. "It won't open, trust me."

He ignored me and went over to the painting again, trying to touch the gold gilt frame. "Maybe we can get out using this. If it got me in here, maybe we can get out."

I tugged on his arm, realizing that maybe we could. I hadn't thought about that before. "Jeremy said it was a portal. Maybe you're right."

"But I was in some dark place with nothing surrounding me. There was nothing else. Maybe if I enter it again…" He moved forward.

"No. Don't even think about it. What if it leads to a place worse than this?"

"I doubt any place could be worse than this." He paused and let out a breath. "He stole my body, Shelly, my life. That's how I ended up here. How could that even happen?"

"He said it was all a part of a plan he had to return to the mortal realm."

He gasped and pointed to the painting. "Look. It's not black anymore."

He and I watched swirling colors turn into shapes on the canvas. Seconds later an image appeared like on a movie screen, and we saw my body lying on a stone tomb. It was what I'd seen earlier in the mausoleum.

"I've been there," I said. "That's the Wickcliff mausoleum."

"What's that sick bastard up to?"

We watched as a grotesque woman replaced the image of my body with a deformed face. Her skin was ghostly white; her teeth yellow-green; her eyes sunken in, black and hollow.

Reed stepped back, horrified. "Who's that?"

"That must be Rachel Wickcliff. My husband Rory told me all about her. Rachel was a defiance of nature. She was sick, deformed and emaciated. She's Jeremy's dead sister."

I put my hand over my mouth as we watched Rachel's horrible face appear again.

"I know what's going to happen," I said. "I heard the whole plan."

He looked at me blankly. "What do you mean?"

"I haven't been able to leave the attic in this body, but I can see things in my mind. I saw Gaul, Pit and Jeremy in your body take mine to the mausoleum. Jeremy has some plan to bring his sister back in me." I grimaced at Rachel's face before us on the painting. "Rory told me that she was Irma's only daughter. Irma never talked about her, and no one ever saw her. There were no pictures of her anywhere in the mansion because Irma was ashamed of her. Supposedly, Rachel had died in the tower bedroom of this house, a room she never left while she was alive because she was so sick and disfigured."

His face curled up from the sight of her. "What was wrong with her?"

"I guess she suffered from an incurable disease that didn't allow her to be in daylight and made her hideous to look at. The Wickcliffs were deeply ashamed of her existence. Her only friend was Gaul, who took care of her until the day she died."

"That's horrible." He shook his head in disbelief and stared at the canvas again horrified.

Midnight's Edge, The Secrets of Sleepy Meadows

I felt more helpless than ever. Jeremy was bad enough, but seeing Rachel's dark spirit before us for the first time made his plan more real and devastating. One Wickcliff returning was enough, but not two. I needed a plan to get out of the attic before it was too late.

Chapter 14

I was more determined than ever to escape the Wickcliff attic. Jeremy had been the one to orchestrate my husband's death, he had forced me to commit suicide, and now he was using my body to return his sister, Rachel, to the mortal realm.

I could see by the look on Rachel's emaciated, sunken in face and cold, lifeless eyes that she was just as sinister as her brother.

Then there was Reed. Although I was grateful for the company, I felt sorry for him. He was another victim of Jeremy's, his mind and body taken over. He was an innocent man, and Jeremy had stolen everything from him. I couldn't stand back and watch him destroy yet another life.

"Do you think we can get out of here using the painting?" I asked Reed.

He shrugged. "I got in here using it, didn't I?"

"I don't think we should do anything until we fully understand how it works. That's Jeremy's painting. It could lead straight to hell for all we know. It's too risky. I won't chance it, at least not yet. I'm learning that I have powers. My spirit body may be stuck here, but my mind isn't. There's got to be another way out of here, and we're going to find it."

He groaned and rubbed his eyes. "I still can't believe what's happening. I thought things like possession only existed in campy, low-budget horror movies. It's almost not reality."

"But it is," I said, putting my hand on his shoulder. "As sorry as I am to say that, it's true."

"But how is it even possible?"

"Have you ever heard of Midnight's Edge? It's when the barrier between the realms disappears, and the spirits of the past, of the dead, can return to life. It only happens at certain points, and it takes someone with a lot of power to be successful at going from one realm to another."

He scrunched his face. "That story's been going around town for years. Some old, crazy crone made it up."

I shook my head. "It's not made up. That's how Jeremy was able to use your body to return."

"But it's my body, my life, not his. How is he strong enough to just take it over?"

"He told me that he learned how to do it from his father. He spent years in the darkness learning how to harvest his powers to be strong enough. That's what makes him dangerous. He's not unstoppable. He has a weakness just like anyone else."

"And I suppose you know what that is?"

"I don't want to get your hopes up, but him inhabiting your body is only temporary. If he's going to stay alive, he needs to inhabit the body of someone from his bloodline, particularly a son. If he can't do that, he'll die. His spirit's vulnerable in that way."

His eyes widened. "You mean I could get my life back?"

"It's possible."

"Why didn't you tell me that before?"

I put my hands on his shoulders. "Calm down. Let's not get too excited, okay?"

He took a deep breath and let it out slowly. "Why would he tell you what makes him vulnerable?"

"He knows I'm stuck here, and he doesn't believe that I'm going to get out. He's cocky, overconfident. He always has been. He doesn't think there's anything I can do to stop him. Underestimating me was a mistake. I'm not the same helpless victim I was when I was alive. I'm not only going to stop him, but I'll make him pay for what he's done to me one way or another."

He put his hand up. "Look, don't take this the wrong way, but that's not exactly reassuring. You don't even know how to get out of here, and you don't want to try the painting. Do you have any other suggestions?"

I put my head down for a moment before making eye contact with him again. "I'm afraid not."

He looked away and then back at me as if he were getting an idea. "You said he needs to inhabit the body of someone who shares his bloodline and that he's looking for his son?"

I nodded.

He rubbed his chin, and his eyes glimmered. "I got it. Sleepy Meadows isn't a sizeable town, Shelly. His son has to be someone that we know."

"You're assuming that he's in Sleepy Meadows. He may not be. We might not know him at all. Even if we did, there's nothing we can do from here."

"If we can find out who Jeremy's son is, then we have a shot at being able to intercede before Jeremy can take control. He dies, I go back, and you can move on. I'll bet you anything that whoever he is, he's not that far away. How many people do you know other than your brother who were born here and left? Nobody ever leaves this place."

I stood there thinking for a moment. What Reed said made sense, but how would we intercede? Suddenly I had a thought. "Kasey," I blurted out.

Reed gave me a peculiar look. "Huh?"

"If Jeremy's son's here, he could be Kasey. His parents died when he was a baby, about the same time that Jeremy and his wife died."

"That doesn't prove anything."

I shrugged. "Maybe not in itself, but we know that Kasey was adopted by Gracey Menze, the same one that told us all the stories about Midnight's Edge. That woman you call an old crone knows a lot more about Jeremy's death than she's letting on. She has to. She knew about Midnight's Edge and so did he. I'm betting that Gracey and Jeremy are connected somehow, and I think that the link between them is Kasey."

"It's hard for me to believe that Kase is that man's son. He's a good man. Sure, I was pissed at him, but he's a decent person."

"Gracey raised him. The Wickcliffs didn't influence him. That's what made him the man he is today. I've got to try to make contact with Kasey again."

He raised a brow. "Again? You mean you have before?"

"I've been able to make contact telepathically with the mortal realm, with my loved ones and friends. I can feel their emotions; I can hear some of their thoughts. Most people can't see or hear me, but Kasey can."

Midnight's Edge, The Secrets of Sleepy Meadows

He rubbed his chin. "So Kasey can hear you? That's why he was acting so strange earlier?"

"Partly, I suppose."

"I want to be able to do it too. Can you teach me?"

"I would if I could, but I'm not exactly sure how it happens. I just started thinking of Ethan and then…" I stopped. I suddenly had a strong feeling.

Reed touched my shoulder, noticing the confused expression that washed over my face. "What is it, Shelly?"

"A stranger is on his way into town." I closed my eyes, and my mind began to wander. I saw a road outside of Sleepy Meadows where a rugged, unfamiliar man around Kasey's age was hitchhiking towards town.

I didn't understand why I was seeing him, but like with Pit earlier, I realized that I could connect with people that weren't necessarily close to me. Because I didn't know this man, I believed that he must be involved with someone I knew and loved. I concentrated as hard as I'd done with Kasey, Ethan, and others. There had to be a reason I was seeing him.

He appeared exhausted and was thinking about how he hadn't seen a car in hours. It was too late for people to be out on the roads. Most were at home in bed. Just when he'd given up hope that anyone would come along, an old Ford pickup truck approached.

"Finally," he said, letting out a heavy sigh. He put his thumb up anxiously and stood there waiting.

The truck came to a halt, and he walked up to it. He opened the door and inside an old man sat, wearing stained overalls and a cruddy baseball cap that covered his gray, greasy hair.

The stranger stood there for a moment staring into the dingy interior.

The driver's eyes bore into him. "Do you need a ride or what? I don't have all night."

He stepped into the truck and put his right hand out. "Thanks for stopping, name's Jason."

The driver didn't accept the gesture. "I don't want to know your life story. I keep to myself and suggest you do the same."

Jason took back his hand and closed the passenger door. The smell of manure surrounded him.

"Where ya headed?" the driver asked.

He gave him a half smile. "Sleepy Meadows."

The driver scowled. "Why in the hell would you want to go there?"

"It's personal. Can you take me or not?"

The driver turned his head forward and stared into the distance. There was an uncomfortable silence for what seemed like minutes as Jason sat patiently waiting for an answer.

"I haven't been to Sleepy Meadows in over 30 years," the driver said finally. "I don't have any desire to go there. I guess that means you're on your own."

"It's only five miles away, and I've already been walking for half the night. I don't have much money, but I can give you a little something." He started fishing in his knapsack.

The driver glared at him, still grimacing. "Your eyes...they're so green."

"So I've been told. Can you take me or not?"

"I'll drive you four miles. You'll have to walk the last one."

"That would be great. I appreciate this."

The man grunted. "I don't even know why I stopped."

"Why did you then?"

"Something told me to pull over. There's something about you...no, it can't be."

Jason's eyes widened. "What can't be?"

"Never mind." The driver shifted the truck into drive and hit the gas. "Let's just go."

It was hot inside the truck, and Jason reached into his knapsack, pulling out a handkerchief. He wiped his forehead.

The motion made the man jerk. "What are you doing?"

He faced him. "Nothing. It's just warm in here. You don't have to be so nervous." He wiped the sweat from his brow again. When he attempted to put the handkerchief back, he dropped his bag, spilling several items.

The driver turned on the interior lights and fidgeted when he saw a deck of tarot cards on the seat. He clutched the steering wheel. "Why do you have those? Ya some kinda witch?"

Jason shoved the cards back into his knapsack quickly and chuckled.

Midnight's Edge, The Secrets of Sleepy Meadows

"I don't believe in witches. These aren't even mine."

"Why do you have them then?"

He hesitated before answering and thought about the gypsy woman who had raised him. Her name was Roxanne, and the cards had been hers. "Sentimental value. They belonged to someone I cared about. Don't worry about it. I'm not some kinda fruitcake."

The driver relaxed a bit and continued to drive. He drove a few miles in awkward silence and then broke the ice. "You never told me why you're goin' to Sleepy Meadows."

Jason glanced out the window lost in thought. "My parents lived there, and I never knew them. I want to know where I came from." He turned his head and studied the driver's face. "What's so wrong with Sleepy Meadows that you're so reluctant to take me there?"

The driver turned his head sharply. "What's wrong? I'll tell ya what's wrong. The people there tend to keep to themselves. It's not a place that gets many visitors. I'd watch your back if I were you."

"You make it sound like some terrible, mystical place. It can't be that bad."

"Oh it is and worse. You'll see. There are places on earth that are marked, and Sleepy Meadows is one of 'em."

"What does that mean?"

"The people who live there don't want outsiders comin' in after what happened there, and that's fine by me."

"What happened?"

The driver's wrinkled face turned beet red. He turned the steering wheel sharply and pulled the truck over in front of a sign on the road that read: Sleepy Meadows, 1 mile ahead. "Anyone ever told you that you ask too many questions? You'd better keep those questions to yourself once you get into town if you know what's good for ya. This is where you get out."

Jason huffed and grabbed his bag. "Fine, but you didn't answer my question." He reached to pull the door handle and stopped when the driver grabbed his other arm, squeezing it hard. The strength of the older man's grip surprised him. He glanced down at his arm and then locked eyes with the man, noticing his intense stare. He tried to pull his arm away, but the driver held on tightly. "What the hell's wrong with you man?"

"Sleepy Meadows isn't an ordinary town. Things have happened there that you can't even imagine. There's tainted soil where evil still lurks. If you don't believe in demons, you will. Be forewarned. There are witches and others who try to keep the evil at bay, but it'll come back. It always does. I guarantee it."

Jason yanked his arm away, which made more items fall out of his bag. "Now look what you made me do." He tried to pick things up and looked back up at the driver. "That's the most ridiculous thing I've ever heard in my life."

The driver turned on the overhead light again and glanced down at the floorboard where the items had fallen out. He noticed a small crystal pendulum laying there and gasped. "You're one of them, aren't you?"

"One of whom?"

"Yes. I can see it now. I can tell by those green eyes of yours. I should've known, but you've probably got me under some spell."

"You're talking nonsense."

"No. You're definitely one of them."

"One of whom!"

"A Wickcliff!"

Jason narrowed his eyes. "A Wickcliff? I've never heard that name. My last name's Beckett."

"Liar!"

"I'm telling you I've never heard of them. Who are they?"

"As if you don't know. I'm sure you're just as demonic as the rest of them. Get out."

Jason's face reddened. "What did you call me?"

The driver pointed to the door. "Get out, I said! I don't need any damn Wickcliffs crossing my path. Leave me alone. Do you hear?"

He put his hands up and took in a deep breath. "Listen, I don't know what you think, but I'm not going to hurt you. I just wanted a ride."

"All the Wickcliffs know how to do is hurt people. I'm sure you know that." The driver released his arm and pointed to the door again. "Now I told you to get outta here. I don't need any of your dark magic influencing me."

He exhaled, grabbed his knapsack promptly, and opened the door.

He jumped out of the truck, slammed the door, and rotated around to face the truck again. Before he knew it, the driver had made a U-turn on the road and sped off, leaving a trail of dust behind. He grumbled and wiped the dirt off his clothes. "What the hell was that all about? That guy must be nuts."

After cleaning himself off, he glanced up at the sign. Although he was thankful that the ride from the crazy old man had gotten him closer to his destination, he was still exhausted and wasn't thrilled about having to walk another mile. He let out a heavy sigh, hefted the knapsack over his shoulder, and stared down the long road ahead of him.

He started walking and thought about what the man had told him. He'd called him a Wickcliff, a name he'd never heard before. All he knew about his childhood was the first name of his mother. Could the man be right? Was his mother a Wickcliff? A curious expression washed over his face as he began the last mile.

* * * *

I was just as curious now. Maybe it wasn't Kasey that was Jeremy's son, but this new stranger. I didn't want the man that I thought of as family to be a Wickcliff. For my own selfish reasons, I wanted the old man to be right. I surmised that maybe that's why I could see Jason. Maybe he was the true Wickcliff heir. I felt Reed tugging on my arm, and I opened my eyes.

"Well, what did you see?"

"I'm not so sure that Kasey's Jeremy's son after all. It could be someone else although Jeremy doesn't need to know that. I see things for a reason, Reed." I smiled widely. "Jeremy doesn't realize it yet, but I think we just got the upper hand."

Chapter 15

I tried to focus my attention back to Jason, but instead what I saw perplexed me. It was Rebecca pulling into her driveway and sitting in her car alone. She'd been a friend once, but I'd cut off contact with her years ago as I had with many others once Jeremy's torture began to take over my life. I didn't understand why my thoughts would gravitate to someone whom I hadn't seen in such a long time.

It looked to me as if Rebecca had been crying, and I soon found out why. She'd been thinking about Ethan and what it felt like to see him again. Seeing Ethan in such a vulnerable state had reminded her of what she'd found so attractive about him.

I didn't know it in life, but now I understood that she'd been in love with my brother and that those feelings still lingered. She'd realized that he didn't return her feelings and had accepted that they could never be together, but it still hurt.

She felt sorry for him because our dad was in the hospital, I was nowhere to be found and because it was obvious that the relationship between Ethan and our mother was strained, to say the least.

She made a vow that from now on she'd be the support system that he was lacking. She hoped he'd stay in town if he had some support, but she didn't understand that the reason he left five years ago was much more complicated than his strained relationship with our family.

It seemed to her that our family was falling apart. Ethan had returned to town just in time to be the glue that held it together, although she suspected that that wasn't a role he wanted to take on.

She got out of her car and approached her front door, feeling nothing but dread because Pit would be waiting for her and probably start a fight, accusing her of sleeping around because she was out late.

She'd known him long enough to know what set his temper off, and although she used to avoid doing or saying things that would upset him, it was getting harder and harder to do so.

At this point in her marriage, she no longer cared. She wasn't in the mood to deal with him anymore, especially tonight and just wanted to take a shower and crash.

She reached for the doorknob and debated whether or not she even wanted to enter the house. It wasn't the fight that she dreaded the most, it was the fact that she didn't love him. She never had.

Marrying Pit was the biggest mistake of her life. At the time, she'd been too young and felt pushed into the marriage for many reasons. He was cruel and verbally abused her, always put her down, and made her feel like she was never enough. Because of that, she'd struggled with her self-esteem for years. She had always considered herself strong-willed and feisty, but now she felt broken down and hopeless. I knew how that felt. Deep down, she wished that my brother could've been her husband.

The lack of love made her marriage a living hell. Pit drank too much and didn't pay any attention to her unless he was in the mood. Even then, she just laid there letting her mind wander until he was finished. Lucky for her it never took him long. She often cringed when he touched her. The nausea was almost overwhelming. He was an insensitive lover, and she made sure it didn't happen often. In fact, it hadn't happened for over a year. She longed to be with a man who would truly make love to her.

She and Pit only fought verbally. He had hit her once, but she responded by punching him in the face and telling him that if he ever hit her again, she'd kill him. He knew she meant it, and he hadn't laid a hand on her since. She might have felt beaten down, but she refused to let Pit literally beat her.

After entering the house quietly, she noticed that Pit wasn't in his favorite chair in front of the TV. She thought that was strange because he rarely moved from that spot. She walked into the bedroom and found him there, clothes thrown all over the place and empty suitcases covering the bed. When she entered, he looked up and saw her standing in the doorway.

"Where the hell have you been, woman?"

She put her hands on her hips. "I told you that I was at the hospital with Ethan. For the last time, my name isn't woman. It's Rebecca."

"Bitch." He turned his head back to the suitcase and muttered some more obscenities.

She tapped him on the shoulder. "Excuse me? You had better hope that I heard you wrong. And what's with the mess? Where are you going?"

He went over to the closet and yanked out some more clothes. "We're leaving. Now shut your trap and start packing your shit."

She turned around and began to walk out. "You can leave if you want to, but I'm not going anywhere with you."

"I don't have time for this. We have to leave Sleepy Meadows tonight."

She turned back around to face him. "What's going on?"

He crammed the clothes in his suitcase. "I can't answer all these questions right now. You gotta trust me."

She snickered. "Trust you? You'd sell your own mother's soul to the devil if it benefited you. I don't trust you in the slightest."

He grabbed her by both arms and started to shake her. "Dammit, Becca. This isn't a joke. If we don't leave now, we're dead. You got it?"

She saw the genuine fear in his eyes but dismissed it. "Are you drunk?"

"No."

"Well, you smell like a brewery."

He released her arms and pushed her back. "I'm not drunk!"

"Don't tell me you're high." She folded her arms. "Are you doing drugs?"

He turned his attention to the bed where clothes lay in clumps. "I wish it were that simple. Drugs are nothing compared to this."

She stood there and watched him throw more clothes in another suitcase still unconvinced of the seriousness in his tone.

"I can't believe she did it," he said. "I never wanted to get involved. Why did he have to call me?" He clenched his fists and slammed them on the suitcase.

She had just about enough and grabbed his arm. "Who did what? Who called you? What did you do, Pit?"

He yanked his arm away and then pushed her. She fell to the floor. "Just shut up. I need to think."

She got up quickly. "You bastard. I told you never to touch me like that again. I told you what would happen." She tried to slap him, but he grabbed her hand.

"You wanna kill me? Go ahead. I'm dead anyway!"

"You're so over dramatic and crazy. I'm tired of dealing with it." She pulled away from him and headed towards the living room.

He followed her. "Where the hell do you think you're going?"

She didn't look back. "Out!"

"You're the one who's crazy. I tried to warn you. If something happens to you, it's your fault. You got that? I'm not going to feel guilty."

She left and slammed the door behind her. She got back in her car and drove to the only place where she could clear her head, the docks that our family used to unload shipments. The water seemed to have a calming effect on her too, just as it had with Ethan.

Once she got there, she stood silently and stared out at the water, trying to regain her composure. Her heart was still beating fast, and she trembled. She started to cry, completely engulfed in her unhappiness with the way life had turned out for her. She was stuck in a loveless marriage with no fulfilling career and no real friends except for Kasey and Ethan, who had just returned after being away for so long. She'd always tried to be a decent person and believed that she deserved to be happy.

"What's wrong?" a man's voice said, disrupting her thoughts.

Startled by the voice, she turned around quickly and wiped her eyes clean.

I recognized the man as the one I'd seen earlier getting a ride from the old man in the pickup truck.

"I'm sorry," Jason said, putting up his hand. "I didn't mean to scare you."

She caught a glimpse of him standing under the lamppost. He looked muscular, strong, with dark, wavy brown hair and the most intense green eyes she'd ever seen. She took a step back. "Who are you? What are you doing here this time of night?"

He put both his hands up, smiled, and started walking closer to her without saying anything. The closer he got to her, the more brilliant the green in his eyes became.

She backed up. "Don't come any closer."

"I'm not going to hurt you, miss."

She felt the railing of the dock pressing against her back. There was nowhere else to go. "How do I know you aren't some sort of attacker?"

He laughed. "Me? An attacker? Hardly. I wouldn't hurt a fly."

"Why else would a man be down here at this time of night?"

He gave her an inquisitive smile. "Well, you're here. Does that mean you're an attacker?"

She dropped her shoulders and sighed. "Don't be cute."

I could tell she thought he was harmless, but I didn't know enough about him to tell for sure. "Truth is I don't have a place to go," he said. "I lost my job with a fishing fleet where I'm from. The company folded, and I came here looking for work. I heard that there was a similar business here."

She gave him a nod. "The Hawkins' Fishing Company."

"Right. That's it. I don't have anywhere to sleep. I don't have much money. I ended up here." He looked off into the distance. "I've always been drawn to the water. It'll be fine; it'll only be for one night. I was planning to talk to the Hawkinses in the morning. I'm hoping that'll go well. If not, I'll go home."

She thought about why she'd come tonight and realized the water drew her here. As she stared at him, she noticed a sad look in his eyes that reminded her of her own. Here she was feeling so sorry for herself when there were people like him worse off than she.

"This was probably a bad idea," he said. "Maybe I should just forget it and try and get home."

She reached out her hand to stop him. "With no money?"

"It took more to get here than I thought. I guess I didn't prepare well."

She stepped even closer. "Look, I know the Hawkins family. Maybe I can help you."

"I can't ask you to do that, Miss...?"

She put her hand out. "Rebecca Wexler...Becca."

As I looked into Rebecca's face, I could see what was happening. She was attracted to him, and that had me worried for her. She had to be if she gave him her maiden name. I wondered what sort of trouble she could get herself into if she got involved with a man who was potentially a Wickcliff.

He returned her handshake. "I'm Jason Beckett."

"It's nice to meet you."

They stood there silently for a moment until his rumbling stomach interrupted the silence. "Sorry, haven't had much to eat either."

She chuckled. "When was the last time you ate, Mr. Beckett?"

"It wasn't that long ago." His eyes fell to the ground, and his stomach rumbled again. "Okay, it was a while ago, a few days maybe."

"Days? Oh my, you really need to eat."

He smiled and gave her a nod. She smiled back at him and thought his smile adorable. She pointed into the distance. "Come on. There's an all-night diner within walking distance from here. Let's get you a hot meal and out of this cold."

After seeing this scene down by the docks, I was more confused than ever. The old man in the truck accused Jason of being a Wickcliff. Was it true or not? If he were Jeremy's son, I doubt that he'd be starving with no place to sleep. Of course, he said he didn't know his family, only his mother's name.

And then there was Kasey. What if he was Jeremy's son? Maybe it was neither of them.

I kept watching, hoping to find some more clues. I followed them to the diner, determined to learn more about this mysterious man.

* * * *

The Golden Crescent diner was quiet, warm, and open all night, the perfect place for two strangers to get to know each another.

"There ya go, hon," Gloria, the waitress, said, putting Jason's burger and fries in front of him. "Rare. Just the way ya wanted. But if ya get sick, remember, we ain't liable."

"I won't get sick," Jason said. "I promise. I eat these all the time, although it's been awhile."

Gloria gave Rebecca a wink, adjusted the pencil in her thick, rolled-in-a-bun hair and walked away.

Jason bit into the raw burger. "This's so yummy. Perfect. Mmm."

Rebecca curled her nose. "It's gross is what it is. That cow's still mooing. How can you eat that? It's almost bloody."

He wiped his mouth with his napkin. "You don't know what you're missing. The meat has flavor." He held it towards her. "Sure ya don't want to try it?"

She sat back and put her hands up. "Yuck, I think I'll pass." She examined her well-done burger and then watched him inhale his food.

He looked up at her and noticed that she was playing with her food. "Something wrong?"

She looked down at her plate and continued playing with her fries. "I'm not hungry, I guess."

"Oh? I hope it's not due to the company."

She looked up, meeting eyes with him. "It isn't that at all. It's a long story."

He took a bite of a French fry. "You wanna talk about it?"

"I don't even know you, Mr. Beckett."

He swallowed. "Exactly. Who better to spill your guts to than a perfect stranger you'll probably never see again?"

She sighed. "I've got stuff going on at home. I'm worried that my husband's going off the deep end."

He sat back and frowned. "That's a shame."

"Not really. He's never been all there to begin with."

He laughed. "I meant that it's a shame you're married."

She met eyes with him, blushed and looked away. He put his hand on the table as if he were reaching for hers. "I'm sorry. I shouldn't have said that."

"It's okay. I say the same thing when I wake up every morning."

"If you aren't happy, why do you stay?"

She shrugged. "It's complicated."

He picked up his burger again. "I'm an idiot. I shouldn't have asked such a personal question."

"I don't mind. It's nice just to have someone intelligent to talk to for a change."

He took a bite and swallowed. "Your husband doesn't talk to you?"

"I said someone intelligent. My husband has the same IQ as the number of brain cells he's got left…two."

He chuckled. "Ouch."

She noticed how his eyes sparkled and thought his smile was infectious. She was staring at him, hoping he didn't notice, but he did.

"What?" He wiped his mouth. "Do I have lettuce in my teeth or something?"

"Sorry. Just daydreaming I guess."

"I hate to bring this up because you've already been so kind, but you mentioned something about being able to get me a job with the Hawkins Company. How well do you know the family?"

"Very well. Their son, Ethan's a close friend. We grew up together."

"Are you sure it isn't an inconvenience, Mrs. Wexler?"

"It's Ms. Wexler. Wexler's my maiden name. But please call me Becca."

"Okay, Becca. Call me Jason."

She reached across the table and put her hand on his. "And it isn't an inconvenience. I'm the one that offered."

He glanced at her hand, which she didn't move. He didn't want her to. "How can I ever repay you for your kindness?"

She took her hand back. "It isn't necessary."

"I have to do something."

"Fine, if you get the job, maybe you can buy me a burger with your first paycheck."

"Only if you order it rare."

She laughed, but her demeanor soon became serious. "I know you said you didn't have a place to stay. I've got an idea."

"I'm fine. I'll go crash down by the docks."

"I can't let you do that."

"I'm not your responsibility, Becca. I'll be fine. I've been through worse, believe me."

"I know a perfect place. The Moonlight Inn. It's cheap, and I've known the owner my whole life."

"I don't think I have enough money."

She put her hand up. "Let me take care of that."

"I should probably refuse, but it is cold outside. I'll pay you back, I promise. Where is it? Can I walk there?"

She picked her car keys up off the table and got up. "Don't be ridiculous, Mr. Beckett—sorry, Jason. I'm not about to leave a new friend out in the cold to freeze to death. I'll take you."

Chapter 16

As I shifted my focus away from Jason and Rebecca, I had an overwhelming sensation that told me Jason wasn't the only one who had come into town tonight. An old friend of Gracey's had been just behind him in her gypsy caravan. She entered town, stopped by Gracey's house, and fell asleep in her caravan thinking that it was too late to knock on Gracey's door.

I remember seeing her around our house when I was a child. Her name's Hildegarde Reyes, but everyone called her Hilda. She'd been a friend of my mother's too, but I hadn't seen her in years, and no one else had either. She'd left town when I was small. I wasn't sure yet why she was back, but it was clear that she wasn't like everyone else. She had abilities similar to mine. I could feel that. Her instincts were telling her that the people of this town were in danger and needed help.

I switched my focus from outside of the house to the inside. By now, the sun was starting to come up. I'd hoped that by me not bothering Kasey any more last night that he'd be more receptive to me today, having got some rest. I'd have to wake him soon, but right now, my thoughts were on his mother.

I could feel Gracey's fear as she lay in bed. She'd spent the previous night tossing and turning, and when she did sleep, nightmares woke her. She'd been dreaming about Jeremy's return, and it consumed her thoughts. I understood much more about Gracey now that I'd crossed over. When we were kids, we all thought she was nothing but an eccentric old woman. Kasey had to defend her often. Now I understood that there was a reason for her behavior. Both she and Hilda had powers that set them apart from other women.

As the first few rays of sunlight peeked through her bedroom window, she realized she would get no more sleep. She sat up, groaned as she put both feet on the floor and slid into her slippers. Although she was frequently bothered by arthritis, the pain was always worse in the morning before she got moving, especially in her bad leg. It didn't make her feel any better getting hardly any sleep either.

She couldn't shake the feelings of immense fear and uncertainty that she felt this morning. She hadn't felt this much dread since Jeremy had been alive and although she hadn't confirmed it yet, her instincts told her that her dreams were more than dreams, Jeremy was back in the mortal realm again. She grabbed her cane and made her way into the kitchen in the back of the small house. Scruffy greeted her with a bark, and once she'd given the dog her breakfast, she put some water into a kettle and put it on the stove.

While the water boiled, she went to the cupboard to choose which tea she'd make. She thought about the natural honey that Kasey had brought her and about how pleasurable it would be in the tea. Just as she reached for the jar, there was a knock on the door. She flinched, jumped back, and dropped the honey jar on the floor.

"Damn."

"Gracey? I heard a crash. Are you alright in there?"

She recognized the voice standing outside immediately as Hilda's, but since it had been so long since the two had seen each other, she didn't believe that Hilda was there. She approached the door cautiously, thinking that Jeremy had found her and that he was using his black magic to pass himself off as a friend so she'd let her guard down and let him into the house.

"Hilda? Is it you?"

"Of course dear. Is everything alright?"

She unlocked the door and opened it, but kept the chain bolted. With the door ajar, she glanced upon what looked like Hilda's face. She was older and looked more withered, but she could tell by Hilda's eyes that she was the same woman she'd known.

"Can I come in?" Hilda said. "It's urgent. I have to talk to you."

She undid the chain on the door, opened it all the way, and stepped aside allowing Hilda to enter. "I'm sorry if my knocking startled you."

"Surprised is more like it." She smiled. "I can't believe you're here."

Hilda returned the smile and embraced her. "It's nice to see you old friend."

Hilda broke the embrace, and the two women stared at each other until Gracey broke the silence. "What has it been since we've seen one another, 15 years?"

Hilda nodded. "About that."

"Well, where have you been? Why haven't we heard much from you?"

"I've been here, there, everywhere."

Her smile faded. "I know that this isn't a social call. You're here for a reason, and I think I know what that reason is."

Hilda nodded. "I imagine you do. We've always had a special bond, you and me. We were always able to tell what was on the other's mind. We'd finish each other's sentences."

She didn't say anything for a moment. She stood there looking at Hilda, trying to take in how much she'd aged since their last encounter. The only thing that was the same was her attire. She still wore a long black shawl draped over her hair, which was now all gray. She still wore her trademark color, midnight blue.

"Are you going to tell me where you've been?" she asked.

Hilda shrugged. "It doesn't matter now. After what happened here, I thought it best to leave the past in the past. I've realized now that, unfortunately, I can't do that." She motioned to the table. "May we sit? I had a long night sleeping in my caravan."

She nodded and pulled out a chair. "You didn't have to do that. You could've knocked on my door last night."

Hilda sat down. "I didn't want to impose."

"You'd never be an imposition." She sat down across from Hilda. "Are you here alone? Where's the rest of the gypsy pack?"

"They aren't here. The reason I'm here has nothing to do with them. It has to do with my past, with our past. You know that, don't you?"

She swallowed. "It has to do with Jeremy, doesn't it? I had nightmares about him all night. I've barely slept."

"They weren't just nightmares. He used Midnight's Edge to return last night."

She took a deep breath and exhaled slowly. "That's exactly what I felt that they weren't just nightmares. Maybe our instincts are wrong.

How can we be sure?"

"I'm sure. I got a visit from Lucy. She told me it would happen."

As I listened to their conversation, the name Lucy struck a chord. I tried to place where I'd heard it before. Then I remembered that Lucy was the name of Jeremy's wife, the one he told me betrayed him. Lucy died with Jeremy in the accident that had taken their lives.

It was becoming apparent that not only did the two women have premonitions and feelings, they also had the ability to communicate with the dead. It made me wonder why they couldn't tell that I was with them. Why could Hilda see and feel Lucy and not me? What sort of connection did the women have that they didn't share with me?

The water in the kettle came to a boil and upon hearing it whistle, Gracey got up slowly, turned it off, and moved the pot to a cool burner. Then she turned back to Hilda and broke the uncomfortable silence. "I can't believe that Jeremy's returned after everything we went through, everything we sacrificed to banish his evil from this world. Lucy gave up her life to save us all. I feel like it was all in vain."

Hilda's facial expression turned morose, and she shuffled in her chair uncomfortably. It was obvious that she was in physical pain. Gracey hated seeing that her health had declined so much in the years they'd been apart.

"We can't get lost in the past and start thinking about what could've been," Hilda said. "We have to concentrate on what's happening now. Jeremy walks among the living, and we have to come up with a plan to get rid of him. I think you need to call your son. We have to have a serious conversation."

She sat back down and shook her head adamantly. "I won't involve Kasey in this."

Hilda took her hand. "You know as well as I do that Jeremy's presence here puts Kasey in danger."

"I know what we both feel, and I know what Lucy told you, but I've got to believe Jeremy's dead for my own sanity's sake."

"Evil never dies dear, you know that. It just changes forms, and the Wickcliffs are capable of many things. We've been blessed with many years of peace, but that's about to come to an end. I can feel it in my bones, and I know you do too, whether you want to admit it or not."

"I know you're right. I trust you, especially after you saved my life during our last encounter with him. I wish you were wrong, but I know you're not." She sighed. "How am I going to tell Kasey the truth after all this time?"

"I know it's hard, but he needs to know where he came from, and what his mother did to save him—to save all of us."

Now I was confused. I'd first thought that Kasey was Jeremy's son, but then I had a suspicion that the new stranger in town, Jason, could also be the Wickcliff heir. After listening to the conversation that Hilda had with Gracey, I was beginning to think that maybe Kasey was Jeremy's true son after all. Why else would he be in danger?

"Thank you for coming here to warn us," Gracey said. "It's good to see you regardless of the circumstances."

Hilda's eyes moistened. "It's been many years, but I never forgot you, and I never stopped caring about you."

Her eyes welled-up. "I can see that in your eyes." She'd missed Hilda too. They had separated long ago, but seeing Hilda now reminded her of how much their separation had hurt them both. She got up from the table and went to the phone.

Hilda's eyes followed her. "Who are you calling?"

"I'm calling Carol. She needs to know what's happening right away."

I wondered why Gracey had to call Mom. How was she involved with Jeremy? Why was it so urgent to notify Mom immediately? Even though things were starting to become clearer, there was still so much I didn't understand.

* * * *

Hearing Gracey and Hilda talk about my mom got me thinking about my family again. My brother was back in town, and I would've given everything to see him and talk to him. It had only been one night since I'd crossed over, and I'd already begun to miss my life. I realized now that no matter how much I felt as if Jeremy had made it unbearable, it was nothing compared to the emptiness I felt knowing that I'd never be able to see my parents, brother, and son. I'd never be able to hug them or tell them how much I love them. At least I could see and hear them even if they didn't know I was there.

I decided to focus my attention on Ethan again. I wanted to try to get through to Kasey, but I realized it was early and if I wanted him to be strong enough to hear me, he needed rest. When my brother came into focus, I saw that he was already awake and out of our parent's house. He'd gone to the meadows where he'd always go to get peace when he needed to be alone.

He was troubled. He was worried about our dad's condition, he wondered what secret our mother was keeping about the Wickcliffs, and he was still worried because he couldn't locate me. Once he left the meadows, he was planning to come to the mansion to look for me, although Pit, Gaul, and Jeremy made sure I wouldn't be found there.

I hadn't realized it in life, but the meadows had been a special place for my brother because of Kasey. They'd gone there to be together in secret, to hide, to escape, to talk about the dreams they shared. It was at the meadows where Ethan had told Kasey about his plan to leave Sleepy Meadows and start a new life. I didn't know it then, but they'd been in love. My brother was gay and had lied to himself and those around him. Kasey wanted the two of them to build a life together, and it didn't happen.

I watched as Ethan went inside the old abandoned house on the property that people had nicknamed the 'love shack' throughout the years. He sat down in an old chair by a dusty, cobwebbed-filled window and began to think about Kasey. He thought about seeing him last night at the hospital and how wonderful that felt. Ethan had shut him out both emotionally and physically, and I could tell that it was killing him. He was in love with Kasey although he didn't want to admit it to himself.

I wished that I could've hugged him. I wanted to tell him that I knew who he was now, that it was okay and that I wouldn't have looked at him any differently. In fact, many people would've probably respected him for being who he was and not hiding it.

He thought about the last time he and Kasey had been in this place together, and how they had made love so gently and tenderly. He smiled as he recalled how loving Kasey had been afterward. It had been the first time that Kasey told Ethan he loved him. Ethan had done the same. It was the only time that either one of them admitted it. He'd been happy then because he finally found someone like him, someone from whom he didn't have to hide. He couldn't deal with his feelings and the happiness that he and Kasey shared that day turned into hopelessness.

Ethan's thoughts were interrupted when he heard the door open. He turned to find Kasey standing in the doorway. Seeing him here in their place made it seem like no time had passed at all.

I knew that this was my chance to connect. I needed to get through to Kasey while he was with my brother.

"What are you doing here, Kase?"

"Tell him, Kasey," I said. *"Tell my brother what I showed you."*

Kasey could hear me, I could tell by the look on his face, but he shut out my voice and focused on Ethan. "I was looking for you. I stopped by your house a while ago, and your grandmother said you left early."

"And you knew I'd be here?"

Kasey smiled and gave him a nod. "This was always the place where you'd come to think. This was our place." He paused, and his smile faded. "Listen, Ethan, I need to talk to you, and I don't quite know where to start. I saw something pretty disturbing last night."

"What is it?"

"I'm not sure you're going to believe me, but I promise you it's the truth. At least I think it is, anyway."

I was getting anxious. He was going to do it. He was going to tell Ethan about the vision I showed him of my hanging. My family had to know the truth about my fate. *"Do it, Kasey. Tell him."*

"Kase, you aren't making any sense."

"I know. I'm having trouble finding the words." He exhaled sharply and looked down. "I don't know if I can."

Ethan put his hand on Kasey's shoulder. "Just tell me. We can tell each other anything."

As Kasey met eyes with my brother and looked into them with compassion, I knew he wasn't going to tell him. He wanted to, but he still wasn't sure that what I'd shown him had been real. Even if he had been sure, he didn't know how he was going to shatter my brother's heart by telling him my fate. He was hoping that going to the police and telling Graham what he thought happened was going to be enough for the truth to be revealed so that he didn't have to be the one to tell Ethan.

Kasey hesitated and then rubbed his Ethan's hand. "I've missed you so much."

Ethan gazed at him, desperately fighting the urge he had to be in his arms. He was tired physically and emotionally and tired of the fight. He put his arms around Kasey and began kissing his face and then his lips.

"Why?" Kasey whispered. "Why did you leave me?"

"Kasey, please. Let's just enjoy this time together."

Kasey didn't say anything, and they kissed tenderly again. After a moment, they were interrupted by Ethan's phone ringing.

Ethan broke away, sighed heavily, and took his phone out of his pocket. "I'm sorry. I have to take this. It might be about my dad."

It was our mom on the other end asking him to come to the hospital to be with Dad because she had been called by Hilda and Gracey. She didn't tell him that. She only said she needed to step out for a while. Ethan ended the call and put his phone away.

"Is everything okay?" Kasey asked.

"I've gotta get back to the hospital. My mom needs to go out, and we don't want to leave Dad alone. Can we talk about what you wanted to tell me later?"

"Sure. I understand that you have to go, but we have a lot more we need to talk about."

Ethan smiled and caressed Kasey's cheek. "Later, I promise."

* * * *

I realized that Kasey's feelings for my brother were going to keep him from telling Ethan the truth about what happened to me. What good is being able to have someone see and hear me if they aren't going to relay my messages? Kasey was too emotionally invested with my brother and with my family to tell them what he saw.

Maybe Jeremy was right. He'd said that there wasn't going to be anyone who was going to be able to help me and, as much as I hated to admit it, it was starting to become more apparent that what he said was true.

Jeremy had been on my mind. I needed to see what he was up to. When he came into focus, I saw that he'd arrived at the hospital and was at the front desk asking where he could find my dad's room.

Midnight's Edge, The Secrets of Sleepy Meadows

The young nurse at the nurse's station recognized him as Reed and smiled widely, batting her eyes. "Hello, Reed, I haven't seen you in a while."

Jeremy hesitated for a second, not knowing how she knew Reed or who she was to him. "Hello, Ma'am," he said, awkwardly.

She laughed and threw her head back. "Ma'am? I'm not that old, am I? You've never called me that before."

He shrugged. "Sorry."

She waved her hand. "Don't worry about it. So how have you been?"

"Fine. Busy."

"I suppose you're here to see your boss? It's a shame about Mr. Hawkins, isn't it?"

Jeremy nodded. "Yes. Yes, it is."

"I normally wouldn't give out this information, but I know how highly he thinks of you. Seeing you may make him feel better." She pointed down the hall. "He's in room 2-b."

He gave her a friendly smile. "Thanks." He started walking down the hall rolling his eyes thinking about how much of a fool she was. He stopped when he saw Ethan walking into Dad's room. He hadn't met him yet. He turned around and went back to the nurse. "Who's the guy that just walked into Mr. Hawkins' room?"

The nurse's brow furrowed. "I know Ethan's been gone for a while, but it hasn't been that long."

He gave her a blank look, not knowing what else to say.

Chapter 17

The nurse raised her right eyebrow and scrunched her face. "Reed, are you alright? You look sort of pale."

He touched his cheek. "I do?" He rubbed his temple. "Had a long night, that's all."

He turned away from her and rubbed his temple again. I could tell that he was beginning to realize that passing himself off as Reed wasn't going to be as easy as he thought, but he wasn't going to give up.

Ethan walked out of Dad's room and approached Jeremy. As he got closer, Jeremy could see the resemblance between father and son. Ethan looked like a younger version of our dad, the man Jeremy had known when he was alive.

"Long time, no see," Ethan said, extending his hand. "How ya been, Reed?"

Jeremy returned the handshake and feigned a smile. "It's been a while. I'd ask you the same thing, but I think I already know the answer." He gestured with his eyes towards Dad's room.

Ethan sighed heavily. "I was hoping that there would be some improvement this morning, but there's no change."

Jeremy tried to act nonchalant and put his hands in the pockets of his jeans. "How bad is it?"

"He had two heart attacks. He's sleeping now, finally."

The sick bastard was taking pleasure in this, but he had to continue to pretend like he gave a damn.

"That's terrible," Jeremy said. "He must be exhausted."

"Actually it's the opposite. He had to be sedated so they could get him to relax."

"Really?" Jeremy tried to hide his intrigue. "Why's that?"

Ethan rubbed his temple and looked away. "He was just talking crazy."

I wanted to scream at Ethan. To warn him and tell him that it wasn't Reed he was talking to. But there wasn't anything I could do. He couldn't hear me.

"Mr. Hawkins has always been a rational kind of man. He's probably just confused."

Ethan shrugged. "Maybe. But I think he believed what he was saying."

Jeremy's eyes narrowed. "What do you mean? What was he saying?"

Ethan waved his hand. "It's not important. It was just a lot of nonsense."

"I'm sorry. I don't mean to interfere. I was just wondering how I could help."

Ethan put his hand on Jeremy's shoulder. "Thanks, Reed, but I don't think there's anything you can do. He's just so out of it right now. He tried to tell me that my sister may be dead."

Jeremy's eyes widened. He was genuinely surprised that our dad may have known. "I don't believe it. Well, she's not dead. I saw her yesterday, and she said she needed to get away."

"You lying son of a bitch! Don't listen to him, Ethan." I was becoming more frustrated by the moment, and there was nothing I could do about it.

Ethan's head went back. "Really? Where was she going? We've been trying to reach her. I was going to go up to the Wickcliffs to talk to her this morning, but then I got the call to come here."

"She didn't say where she was going, but she looked alright. She'll be back."

"That doesn't sound like her." Ethan stared off into the distance. He had no reason not to believe who he thought was Reed, but nothing added up. "There's nothing I can do about it right now, I guess. I just wish she would've told someone."

"At least you know that she's okay." Jeremy watched his expression. "What else did your father say?"

"This one's worse. He said something about the Wickcliffs returning from the grave to get revenge on our family."

I wanted to scream. Now that Jeremy knew that my dad was putting all the pieces together, there was no telling what he'd do to him. Jeremy had done away with me, now he was probably going to go after our father, and I was helpless to stop it. Jeremy chuckled. "Revenge for what?"

"Hell if I know. Like I said, he was talking crazy."

"It does sound ridiculous."

"Doesn't it?" Ethan yawned and covered his mouth. "God, I'm beat."

Jeremy saw an opportunity and jumped on it. He put his hand on Ethan's shoulder. "You look exhausted. Why don't you get a coffee or soda?"

Ethan glanced back at our dad's room. "I can't leave him."

"I'll stay. It'll be okay. Besides, I'd like to tell him that I'm praying for him."

My heart sank at the prospect of Dad left alone with Jeremy, but all I could do was observe.

"Okay," Ethan said, still not sure if he should leave. "I'll only be gone for a minute. I'll tell the nurse that you'll be in here with him."

"Great." Jeremy smiled deviously as he watched Ethan walk over to the nurse's station. After Ethan had left, he turned and entered Dad's room. I could tell from the expression on his face that he thought Dad appeared weak and pathetic laying there in the bed and that what he had planned for him was going to take no effort at all.

He stood by his enemy's bed quietly and watched him sleep. It was as I had feared, he knew that Dad knew the truth, and that put my father in grave danger. It was as if Dad sensed that Jeremy was there because he blinked several times and then opened his eyes. "Shelly, is it you?"

"I'm here, Daddy," I said, knowing he couldn't hear me. *"I'm with you. You were right about Jeremy. He's here. That's not Reed. Please, you have to know the truth."*

Jeremy leaned in closer to him. "No, Jeffrey. It's not Shelly."

Dad tried to focus his eyes. "Reed? What are you doing here?"

"We need to have a chat, just you and me, you old bastard."

Dad's brow furrowed. "What did you call me?"

"You heard me."

Dad squirmed in the bed uncomfortably. "Reed would never talk to me like that. Who the hell are you?"

"Don't you recognize me, Hawkins?"

Dad shook his head, and then his face tightened.

"I'm deeply hurt," Jeremy said. "Our families go back such a long way."

Dad's eyes bulged. "You need to leave. I'm not well, and I don't have time for these games."

Jeremy held up one finger. "Maybe just one. Who did you know that was rich, handsome, charismatic and was killed because his whore of a wife betrayed him?"

Dad's chest tightened. "Good God in heaven! Jeremy, it is you. I knew you'd come back."

"Good guess. You're not as dumb as you look."

"Lucy didn't betray you. She was a hero, giving up her life to make sure the rest of us had peace. She rid you of this world."

"The bitch got me, yes, but she also lost her life in the process. I'm alive, she's not. I guess in the end I won after all."

"What did you do to my daughter? Where is she?"

"She told you what was going to happen when you talked to her, didn't she?"

Dad's voice lowered. "You killed her?"

"Not exactly. She did it for me."

Tears formed in Dad's eyes. "Oh, dear God."

"He can't help you now. You tried to warn Ethan about me. Lucky for him he thinks you're nuts."

Dad tried to push himself up on the bed. "Stay away from my son, you psychotic son-of-a—"

"That isn't a very nice way to talk to the person who holds your life in his hands."

Dad's face went pale. "What do you mean?"

"Well, nobody believes you now. But in time, they may. I can't have you running your mouth and ruining my plans. That would be no fun at all."

"What are you going to do?"

"That's none of your concern now. You see, your life as you know it is over. Just like your daughter's."

"No... I'm not going to let you get away with this. I don't know how the hell you got here or what you've done to Reed, but I'm going to make sure everyone knows who and what you are." Dad reached for the call button on the side of the bed.

Jeremy grabbed the device out of Dad's hand and then raised his other hand and made a fist. "I've had it with the sound of your voice." He tightened his fist more. "Do you feel that? It's only a little pressure at first, right?"

Dad put his hand over his heart and gasped for air. His face turned red. "I can't...breathe."

Jeremy cackled. "That's the point. Do you feel the pain, Hawkins?"

I looked on as Jeremy tortured my father. *"Please stop,"* I said, hoping Jeremy could hear me. *"I'll do whatever you want, but leave my father alone."*

Dad writhed in the bed. "Stop, I beg you."

"It's excruciating, isn't it?"

Dad clutched his chest with one hand and tried fruitlessly to grab the call button out of Jeremy's hand with the other. He gasped and then tried to yell for help, but he couldn't get the words out.

Jeremy leaned on the bed. "Don't be afraid, Hawkins. Don't fight it. It's too unbearable. The pain makes you think your heart will burst. Until eventually," he snapped his fingers, "it just stops."

Dad's eyes widened, and he gasped, sat up, and then fell back on the pillow with panic-filled eyes. In a matter of seconds, his face softened, his head fell to the side, and his heart monitor flat-lined.

"No, Daddy!" I began to cry and wondered why I was shown this. If they can't hear me, and if I can't intervene, what was the point?

Jeremy straightened his back, smiled devilishly and then ran to the door. "Help! Someone help us!"

Before anyone else came in, he walked back to Dad's bed calmly and whispered softly in his ear, "mission accomplished."

Horrified and not knowing what to do, I turned my attention back to Ethan. Jeremy had already taken my life, now he had taken our father's too, and my brother needed to know.

Ethan had just opened his soda near the vending machines when he heard a voice boom over the loudspeaker announcing a code blue. The announcement startled him, and he dropped the soda can on the floor. He didn't want to believe it was Dad and hoped that it was someone else, but he knew better even though he didn't want to admit it. He raced to Dad's room and the closer he got, the more I could feel his sense of dread grow.

When he got there, he saw Dr. Marsh inside the room with a nurse. He turned around and saw Jeremy at the end of the hall with a strange expression on his face; Ethan caught him smirking and rushed over to him.

"What happened?" he asked.

Jeremy put a hand on his cheek acting dumbfounded. "I don't know."

I wanted to tell him that Jeremy murdered our father. That he had to open his eyes and see that he wasn't Reed.

He threw his hands up. "What do you mean you don't know? He was fine a minute ago!"

"We were just talking, and then he took a breath and the monitor flatlined. I don't understand."

He went back to Dad's room. A few minutes later, Dr. Marsh came out of the room and removed his disposable gloves.

"What's going on?" he asked.

Dr. Marsh shook his head. "I'm so sorry, Ethan. We did everything we could. There was just too much damage to his heart."

He heard the words but couldn't process them. "Are you trying to tell me…?"

Dr. Marsh put his hand on Ethan's shoulder. "Your father didn't make it."

He took a deep breath and let it out sharply. "Was it another heart attack?"

Dr. Marsh nodded. "The two previous attacks weakened his heart to the point where it just couldn't beat anymore."

"I see." Ethan bowed his head.

"Where's your mother?" Dr. Marsh dropped his hand from Ethan's shoulder. "I'll find her and break the news. You shouldn't be alone right now."

"She isn't here. She left. I was supposed to be watching him. This is my fault."

"That's not true. There's nothing that any of us could've done. God knows we tried."

He met eyes with the doctor. "I need a few minutes alone."

"Take as much time as you need."

Dr. Marsh walked away, and he buried his face in his hands.

Jeremy approached him. "Ethan, if there's anything I can do—"

He removed his hands from his face and stared at him, not seeing him or acknowledging his presence. Instead, he walked away and went into our dad's room.

Dad looked like he was sleeping. All the tubes and wires had been removed. He pulled up the chair next to his bedside, sat down, and took Dad's hand in his. He began to cry.

"It wasn't supposed to be like this, Dad. I promised you that you would get better. I'm so sorry that I couldn't keep that promise. We were supposed to have time to make up for all the years we missed. Why couldn't you fight? You weren't supposed to leave us, goddamn you!"

He put his head on Dad's chest, and his tears turned into heaving sobs. "You had no right to die on us. No right at all. I'll never forgive you for giving up." He began to cry harder, then said, "I didn't mean that. You were always the strong one. I know you fought like hell. I always thought you were strong enough to overcome anything." He let out a heavy sigh. "Remember when I was a kid and Mom would have me wake you up from your naps? Remember what I used to say? I'd say, 'Daddy, wake up for me, please.' Do you think it would work now, Dad? Come on, wake up for me, Daddy…please." He grabbed Dad violently. "Please!" He fell back onto him weeping, laid there for several moments, and then kissed his forehead. "I love you, Dad."

It was difficult to see my brother in this much pain. I wanted to let him know that I was with him, that I was hurting too and that Dad was going to be okay now. He stayed in the room for a few more minutes, wiped his tears, and returned to the hallway. He couldn't stay in the hospital any longer. He felt like the walls were closing in on him, and he needed to escape. He ran out of the hospital to his car, almost blinded by tears, and drove back to the meadows.

I followed my brother there. He was emotionally distraught, and I had to make sure he was alright. Although he couldn't see or hear me, it made me feel slightly better to see him and comfort him in my own way.

As he walked down the familiar path to the Love Shack in the meadows, it came into view in the distance. He started to think about Kasey again and how genuinely safe and loved he felt when they'd been there together. After what happened to our dad, he needed that comforting feeling. He entered the house and heard Kasey's voice behind him.

"I was hoping you'd come back."

Ethan turned around, saw him and smiled.

Kasey smiled back. "I thought I'd stick around for a bit just in case. I'm glad I did."

"I am too."

Kasey looked into Ethan's bloodshot eyes and could tell that he'd been crying. "What happened?"

Ethan bowed his head. "My dad didn't make it."

"Oh God, Ethan, I'm so sorry."

He pulled away when Kasey tried to embrace him. "Don't. Please, I'm okay."

"No you're not."

He put his hands up. "I can't do this right now. There are so many arrangements that need to be made. I haven't even told my family yet. I came straight here."

Kasey came closer. "Ethan, stop. Just stop."

He couldn't hold the grief back any longer and let Kasey hold him in his arms. "I never got to say goodbye, Kase. I wanted to tell him how much I loved him."

"He knew how much."

He looked up at him. "You think so?"

"I know he did."

He laid his head on Kasey's shoulder.

"Everything's okay, Ethan." Kasey caressed him lovingly. "I've got you, and I'm not going to let you go."

Kasey knew for sure now that he couldn't tell Ethan what I'd shown him. Before he'd learned about my father, he was afraid of hurting Ethan and that he wouldn't be believed. Now Kasey thought Ethan couldn't handle any more unpleasant news. All he wanted to do now was comfort him.

Ethan separated himself from Kasey after a moment and wiped his eyes. "I'm okay. I just need to pull myself together."

"Your dad just died. It's okay to fall apart."

He tried to smile through his tears. "You're truly amazing. I thought you'd hate me for leaving you as I did."

Kasey put his hand on Ethan's cheek. "I could never hate you."

He walked over to an old bench and sat down.

Kasey sat next to him. "What are you thinking about?"

"He'll never know. He'll never know the truth."

Kasey knew what he meant. He was talking about being gay. He put his hand on Ethan's shoulder. "I'm sure he did, and he loved you anyway."

"But I never told him. I've lived a lie." He lowered his head.

"It's going to be okay." Kasey caressed his arm. "I love you and I always will. You're my best friend and more. I'm going to give you a piece of advice, though. You can't be happy until you're honest with yourself and those you love about who you are. You can't change it, you have to accept it. It'll be a big burden off your shoulders. Believe me, I know."

He ran his hands through his hair. He stood up and walked over to the window, looked out at the meadows, and then back at Kasey. "It's not that cut and dry for me, Kase."

Kasey stood up too. "I didn't think it would be for me either, but there comes a time when you have to face it."

"That's not what I was talking about."

"Remember the time we first kissed? You didn't talk to me for a week and never mentioned it again. You have a tendency not to face things. Now I understand why you felt like you had to leave."

He laughed. "That's what you think? That I ran away because I couldn't face being gay?"

Kasey took his hand. "You're afraid, Ethan, but you don't have to be. We're together again, and you don't have to face things alone anymore."

He didn't know how to tell him what had happened the night Rory died, the night that he and I had told the police that Rory committed suicide. We thought at the time we were protecting each other, but now I understood what truly happened that night, although he couldn't remember everything. What he remembered was that he thought I'd killed Rory, and that's why he ran. He was afraid if he stayed in Sleepy Meadows, he might slip up and tell someone that I murdered Rory. Neither he nor Kasey realized that they were keeping secrets from each other.

"You're right," Ethan said. "I'm glad you're here."

Kasey smiled. "I have something to show you. I don't know how you're going to feel about it, but I need you to see it."

Ethan looked down at Kasey's crotch playfully. "Right now? I've seen it before."

Kasey jabbed him and laughed. "No, it's not that. This is something much, much bigger."

Chapter 18

They went outside, and Ethan got on the back of Kasey's bike. Kasey took him to his place a couple miles away and parked in front of his trailer.

When they got there, Ethan got off the bike and looked up at a framed building that stood next to the trailer. "Who's building the house?"

Kasey smiled proudly. "I'm building it."

"Impressive." Ethan stood there and admired the work he'd done.

Kasey beamed with pride. "I know it doesn't look like much now, but I've done a lot of the work myself. I can only afford to do so much at a time."

"You did all this?"

"I had some help from the guys in the band, but most of it I've done on my own."

Ethan grinned. "I can't believe it."

Kasey hit him on the shoulder. "Don't sound so shocked, Hawkins."

"No, really. It's beautiful, a lot of work for one person." He noticed that Kasey's expression had turned melancholy and that he was staring off into the distance. "Hey, what is it?"

Kasey turned to him, and his eyes welled up. "It's always been my dream to build a home of my own. You've been part of that dream too."

He put his hand on his chest. "Me? How?"

"I've always hoped that you'd come back and that we'd live here together."

He saw the disappointment in Kasey's eyes and put his arm around him. "Please don't be sad, Kase."

"Why did you have to leave? Our lives could've been so different. We could've been so happy together."

He rubbed Kasey's back. "I never meant to hurt you."

"Did running away from here help?"

"I never stopped thinking about you. I'd lie awake wishing that you were there next to me, that I could be in your arms."

"Then why do you keep pushing me away?"

"Because we can't be together. I can't be gay."

Kasey grabbed his arm. "Why do you deny who you are? It isn't a choice, Ethan."

"It is for me."

"I know you. You can't keep living this lie. It's going to eat you up alive. What happened to your dad put a lot into perspective for me. Life's fragile, and it's short. We've gotta go after what we want while we have the opportunity. You deserve to be happy, we both do. I know what it is you want, and I think you do too."

"Why are you doing this to me?"

Kasey put both hands on Ethan's shoulders and shook him. "Because I love you, dammit! And I know that you love me. I know you remember the way things used to be."

His face went red. "What do you want from me?"

"You! I just want you."

As I watched Ethan and Kasey stand there with tears in their eyes, it reminded me of how I used to look at Rory before Jeremy took everything away from us. It was pure, true love, and it saddened me that my brother and the man I looked at as a brother had been apart when they were so obviously meant to be together. As they looked into each other's eyes, Kasey kissed him passionately and then stopped.

Ethan was breathless. "What is it? What's wrong, Kase?"

Kasey caught his breath and turned away. "We shouldn't do this right now. Your father just died, you're grieving, and we're both vulnerable."

"You just said I needed to go after what it is I wanted."

"Yeah, but we don't have to rush it."

"Stop. Stop talking and stop thinking. We've waited so long. I don't want to wait anymore."

Kasey faced him again. "We can't—"

He put his finger to Kasey's lips and took Kasey by the hand, leading him inside. I looked away for a while knowing what came next. By the time I looked back, they had finished making love and were holding one another. I was happy for Ethan and Kasey too. Despite what had happened to our dad, Ethan was able to find happiness if only for a little while.

"Do you need to go see your mom?" Kasey asked.

"I should. I need to talk to her about Dad, but I'm happy for the first time in such a long time. I'm dealing with so much. I just can't face it right now. Can I just stay with you for a while?"

Kasey pulled Ethan closer to him. "Anything you want."

Before they knew it, they had fallen asleep in each other's arms.

* * * *

"I want to know what's going on, Shelly," Reed said, disrupting me from my thoughts.

I looked at him blankly. "What?"

"I want to know what you're seein. You've been just standing there with your eyes closed. I can see the expressions on your face. What is it?"

Reed had feelings for Kasey. I wasn't about to tell Reed what I saw between my brother and him. "My father's dead. Jeremy murdered him, and he thinks he can get away with it."

His eyes filled with compassion. "I'm sorry. Mr. Hawkins was my boss and a nice man."

I nodded. "That he was. Jeremy's not going to get away with this. I'm going to make sure he's stopped. If my current situation's good for anything, it's that maybe my newfound abilities can help me get the upper hand on him. He doesn't hold all the power anymore."

"What's he doing now? I want to know what he's using my body for."

"It's probably best if you don't know."

"Please, Shelly? It's necessary for me to know. I'll go crazy if I don't. When I think of the things he's making my body do—"

"Alright. I'll try."

I closed my eyes, took a deep breath, and tried to focus on Jeremy's essence. As the picture became clearer in my head, I realized that it wasn't Jeremy that I was seeing, it was Graham Withers.

"Well?" Reed asked.

"I see your father. Now please be quiet, I need to focus."

I shut Reed out and focused all my attention on what I saw before me. Graham had entered the hospital, and I could feel that he wasn't in the best spirits. He was thinking about the events of last night. How he'd come to my house looking for me only to find my car missing, but my purse with all my money, ID, and credit cards still there. As if that weren't enough of a mystery, he couldn't shake the bizarre feeling he had when he approached the gates to the cemetery. He had no idea what evil lurked inside, but he could feel it, and it had scared him enough to leave the premises.

He'd come to the hospital hoping to find my brother and mother and that they would tell him that I'd been located. I could feel his compassion for us. He felt bad about my dad's condition and the fact that I was missing. As I saw Dr. Marsh approach him with a somber expression on his face, I realized that he was about to learn of my father's fate.

"Alex? What's wrong?" He paused. "It's Jeffrey, isn't it?"

Dr. Marsh put his hand on the back of his neck and rubbed it. "I'm afraid so. You haven't seen Carol around here, have you? I had the unfortunate task of telling Ethan, but I haven't seen Carol."

"I'm looking for her too." He exhaled. "I'm sorry to hear about Jeffrey. I was hoping for a better outcome."

"So was I, but sometimes there's only so much that can be done. I saw your boy here a while ago. He was with Jeffrey when he died. He's the one that called for help."

His eyes widened. "Reed was there?"

Dr. Marsh scanned the hallway. "You may want to touch base with him. I noticed he looked pale. He's probably just shaken up, but it wouldn't hurt for him to get checked out."

"I'll do that."

"Excuse me, Graham. I've got rounds." Dr. Marsh walked away.

Hearing Reed's name reminded him of what Kasey had told him about his son being on the Wickcliff grounds in the middle of the night with Pit Bowen. Between not being able to find me and my father's death, he'd almost forgotten. He was already concerned that Reed was hanging around with Pit, and now he'd learned that his son wasn't looking well and was growing worried about him.

His phone rang, and he pulled it out of his pocket to look at the caller ID. At the same time, Jeremy bumped into him. "Hey, watch where you're going."

He made eye contact with Jeremy, not understanding why the man he thought was his son looked at him as if he were a stranger. "Reed, Where are you going in such a hurry?"

"Huh?"

"You came at me like a bat outta hell."

Jeremy gazed at him blankly and shook his head. "I don't…"

He put the phone back in his pocket, letting the call go to voicemail. He grabbed Jeremy's arm and studied his demeanor. "What's wrong with you?"

"I'm sorry, do I—" Jeremy stopped himself realizing that he obviously knew Reed.

He glared at Jeremy. "Where were you last night?"

"Uh…"

"I know what's got you so shaken up. I heard about Jeffrey, and that you were in the room with him when he died. That had to be hard for you."

Jeremy lowered his head. "It was. I'm out of it I guess. I'm sorry."

He rubbed Jeremy's arm. "No need to be sorry, son. Dr. Marsh seems to think you don't look so hot and, judging by those black circles under your eyes, I'd have to agree. Did you sleep at all last night?"

Jeremy's demeanor changed once he realized how he and Reed knew one another. Jeremy relaxed his shoulders and managed a smile. "I'm fine, Dad. I'm just overwhelmed by what happened to Mr. Hawkins."

"I'm sure. It wouldn't hurt for you to be checked out just to make sure you're okay."

"I can't right now. I'm late for an appointment. I gotta go."

Jeremy darted away before he could say another word. He called out to him, but Jeremy didn't turn around. He tried to convince himself that his son was shaken up because of my dad's death and that Dr. Marsh was right about him looking ill because of it. He wanted to believe there was a simple explanation for Reed's behavior, but there was a part of him that told him his son was in trouble. If Kasey was right, and Reed was mixed up with Pit Bowen, it wouldn't end well, and he was going to make sure that he put a stop to that association. He had no idea that Pit was the least of Reed's problems, and that if Jeremy succeeded in bringing the Wickcliffs back to the mortal realm, it wouldn't only be his son who was in danger.

He hung around the hospital for a little while longer and saw neither my mom nor Ethan. He figured that he would give them time to grieve before tracking them down and asking them questions about me. He hoped for their sakes that I'd been in touch with them by now.

* * * *

I opened my eyes, and Reed was there waiting for me to tell him about his father.

"What happened?"

My eyes softened. "Your father saw Jeremy."

"My dad's not an idiot. He had to know that he wasn't me."

I shook my head. "He wants to believe that you're shaken up because he thinks you saw my dad die, but he knows there's more to it than that."

"He'll figure out that freak isn't me."

"I hope so because we're running out of options here."

* * * *

After seeing what impact our dad's death had on my brother, I wanted to turn my attention to Mom. She didn't know about Dad yet, but I knew that it was only a matter of time before she found out the news, and I felt as if I had to be with her when she did.

Hilda and Gracey were confident that Jeremy had returned to the mortal realm and had her over so they could discuss it. I wanted to see how she'd react to the news. It was clear after listening to the conversation that Dad had with Ethan, that Mom knew more than she let on about Jeremy and what happened in his past.

When Mom got to Gracey's house, she went to the back door and, without knocking, entered her kitchen where she found Gracey sitting alone at the table calmly sipping tea.

Mom exhaled, slightly agitated. "This doesn't look like an emergency, Gracey. You said that it was urgent, and it had to do with Jeremy. I left my critically ill husband's side to come here."

"It is an emergency," Gracey said. "I'm just trying to remain as calm as I can. Is Jeffrey any better this morning?"

"He was resting comfortably when I left. Thanks for your concern."

Gracey gestured to her table. "Why don't you sit down so we can talk? Would you like some tea?"

"No, thank you. I can't stay long. I have to get back to the hospital." Mom looked around the room. "Where's Hilda? You said she was here."

"I'm right here, dear." Hilda entered the kitchen from the living room and locked eyes with Mom, giving her a smile. "Hello, Carol. It's good to see you. I'm so sorry to hear about what's happened to Jeffrey."

Mom's face tightened. "Are you?"

Hilda's smile faded. "Why yes."

"Why would you be? You disappeared fifteen years ago, Hilda, and we haven't heard a word from you since. It's been so long I hardly recognize you. It's a little late to be concerned for my family's welfare."

"This isn't the time to do this, Carol," Gracey said. "She's got news that concerns us both."

Hilda put her hand up. "It's alright, Gracey. Let her say what she wants to say."

"What do you know about Jeremy?" Mom said, not taking her eyes off Hilda or letting up on her tone. "That's all I care about, considering the situation."

"You're obviously angry with me."

Mom put her hand on her hips. "You left us and never looked back."

Hilda sighed. "I know you're upset, Carol, but once Jeremy was gone, there was no reason for the gypsies to stay here. My place was with them at that time."

"And now it isn't?"

"Not now. I'm needed here."

"We've always needed you here." Mom sighed. "We were supposed to be your sisters. I thought we were family. I guess I was a fool."

"We are a family. That's never changed, and you aren't a fool." Hilda looked away from her and at Gracey. "I need to sit." She shuffled over to the table, took a seat next to Gracey and looked at Mom again.

Mom scoffed. "A call, a letter, something in fifteen years would've been better than nothing. It doesn't matter now. What are you doing here? What do you know about Jeremy?"

Hilda took in a deep breath. "He's come back to the mortal realm. I don't know in what form yet, but he has."

"How do you know?"

"Our dear Lucy came to me in a vision. He used Midnight's Edge to return and now he's back. I had to come and warn you both. We have to figure out what form he's taken and put an end to him once and for all."

"Why would Lucy come to you and not the rest of us?"

"Maybe because I haven't given up the craft."

I didn't know what Hilda meant by the craft, but it was obvious the three of them shared a past that involved more than friendship.

Mom was going to respond, but her cell phone rang. She took it out of her purse and glanced at the number. "It's Dr. Marsh. I have to take this."

She listened to Dr. Marsh tell her that Dad suffered another heart attack and that this time there was nothing that they could do. Her face turned wan, and her heart sank, realizing that her husband of thirty-five years had just died. She ended the call silently and met eyes with the women again.

Gracey knew the look on Mom's face. "What's happened?" Mom sat down and almost fell out of the chair. Gracey got up and put her hand on Mom's shoulder. "Is it Jeffrey?"

Mom took in a deep breath exhaling slowly and nodded. "He had another attack and passed just a short time ago."

Gracey frowned. "Oh darling, my heart breaks for you. I'm so terribly sorry."

"I'm sorry too," Hilda said. "Whether you believe it or not, I still care for you and your family."

Mom put her hands over her face for a moment, then removed them and stared at the women. "I don't understand how this could've happened. I just left him, and he was fine. He was weak, but he was stable. How can he just be gone?" She stood up. "I have to go. I still don't know where Shelly is, and I have to find her."

"Jeremy has something to do with this," Hilda said. "I can feel it in my bones. The Hawkinses and the Wickcliffs have always been bitter enemies. It isn't a coincidence that Jeffrey's illness and death occurred around the same time Jeremy returned to this world."

Gracey gazed at Hilda. "We can't be positive that Jeremy was responsible for this."

"I think Hilda's right," Mom said. "Jeffrey was on his way to see Shelly at the mansion last night when he had his attack. He never made it there. He told me yesterday that he thought Jeremy was coming back and that he may have done something to Shelly. I didn't want to believe him, but now I know that I should have. If he was right about Jeremy's return, it means that he was probably right about Shelly being in danger too. I can't bear to think…I've got to make sure she's alright."

Gracey touched Mom's arm tenderly. "Let's not get too ahead of ourselves. We don't know that anything's happened to Shelly."

"Jeremy and Jeffrey were bitter enemies. That bastard finally succeeded in getting what he wanted. I know he's responsible for Jeffrey's death, and now he could be going after my daughter."

"Jeffrey's been having heart trouble. It could've just been natural causes."

"Don't be fooled," Hilda said, getting up. "Jeremy's come back for revenge. He still thinks that Jeffrey's father was responsible for his father's death, and he would never let that go. What's happened to Jeffrey is only the beginning."

Mom turned her head sharply in Hilda's direction. "Why didn't you warn us sooner? Maybe we could've stopped him. Now my husband's dead thanks to that madman. This is your fault."

"That isn't true," Gracey said, stepping in between them. "And I won't have you blaming Hilda in my home."

Mom covered her face with her hands again and groaned. After a moment, she removed them and gazed at Hilda. "I'm sorry. I didn't mean that. I've been so hostile towards you since I arrived. It's not your fault. None of this is. I just don't want to face the truth. I never do." She walked over to the back door and glanced out at the backyard. She stared outside lost in thought and then turned back around. "I feel like my whole life's crumbling down around me. My husband's dea. My son hates me. I can't find my daughter. I feel responsible for all of this."

"Ethan doesn't hate you," Gracey said. "Shelly will turn up. You'll see."

"I just don't know what to do now. I suppose I'll have to call Graham about Shelly, but how do we protect the family we have left when we don't even know what we're facing? We don't know what form he's taken and we don't know how much stronger his powers have become since he's been on the other side." She sighed heavily. "Lucy gave her life to make sure that he was destroyed, and now he's back again. What if her sacrifice was for nothing?"

Gracey took her hand. "We need to stick together like we did so many years ago, start figuring out where he is, whom he inhabits, and what he plans to do next."

Hilda nodded. "I agree." She put her hand on the center of the table and gestured to Gracey and Mom to put their hands on top of hers. "We must make a pact to band together to fight Jeremy with every spell, wish, intention, and ounce of power that we have inside of us."

Gracey put her hand over Hilda's and motioned to Mom to do the same. Mom hesitated.

"Carol we need you," Hilda said. "Please join us."

Mom shook her head. "I can't. I haven't used my powers since we lost Lucy. I'm not a witch anymore."

I couldn't believe what I just heard. My mother had referred to herself as a witch. I worried that she'd snapped after hearing about my dad. That had to be it. There were no such things as witches.

"In your heart you are," Gracey said. "That hasn't changed, and it never will. You were blessed with certain gifts and those gifts don't die."

"I'm afraid. We barely escaped with our lives last time."

"Without you we don't stand a chance," Hilda said. "If you agree that Jeremy was behind Jeffrey's death, fight him in your husband's honor. Do it to protect your children and your family."

Mom gave her a closed smile and then joined hands with them.

When all their hands were touching, Hilda began to chant. "We ask for the powers of the Earth, Moon, Sun and the Stars. We ask the elements of Air, Fire, Earth and Water. To the ghosts that walk the Earth among us and to all those young and old. Come and hear the blessed words that leave my lips. Bless us. Make us strong. Blessed be."

Mom's fear began to melt away as she listened to Hilda's words. The ladies watched a glowing circle of light radiate from their hands that soon surrounded them. The warm, comforting glow reminded Mom of how strong and powerful she'd once been. It had been decades since she'd used her powers, but she hadn't forgotten how. Jeremy may have taken her husband, but she was determined that he wouldn't take anyone else away from her. Little did she know that he'd already been responsible for my death.

I was astounded by what I'd just witnessed. My mother really was a witch. I'd never believed in witches. Now I was learning more about her and her coven from the other side. My family had so many secrets. Some things I was grateful to learn while others I didn't want to accept at all.

At least now, Hilda, Gracey, and Mom knew that Jeremy was alive and that he'd killed my father. Now I knew that they'd battled once before, but I didn't understand what happened then.

I wondered if their powers were strong enough to defeat him or if he'd become strong enough to destroy them as he did me and my father. I began to worry for my family's safety more than ever.

Chapter 19

I decided that I needed to keep my focus on my mom. I'd learned that she not only knew about Jeremy and his past but that she had another life that I knew nothing about. I had to find out what else she knew and what she planned to do about Jeremy.

It was noon by the time Mom got back to the hospital and met with Dr. Marsh in his office. He motioned to a chair across from his desk, and she sat down.

"Thank you for coming, Carol. I'm very sorry for your loss. I hope you realize that we did everything we could."

"There wasn't anything you could've done medically to save him. There was another power at work here."

Dr. Marsh folded his hands on the desk. "You mean God?"

"Not exactly."

He stared at her for a moment, clearly not understanding what she meant. "I'm sorry to bring this up now, but there's some paperwork that you need to sign. We need to know where to release the body to."

"I'll take care of it."

"It doesn't have to be right this minute. Jeffrey's body's still in his room. I instructed the staff to leave everything as it was until all the family has had a chance to say goodbye."

Mom got up from the chair. "That's very kind, thank you, but that isn't my husband anymore. It's just a shell. There's not much more I can do here. I'll sign your forms and then I've got to go."

"Carol, forgive me if I've overstepped, but I think that you need to say goodbye to your husband before you do anything else. Many people find that getting the closure helps with the mourning process." He stood up. "It's up to you of course."

"I'll go," Mom said.

They left his office, and he led her down the hallway to Dad's room before leaving her alone. Mom entered the room and saw Dad lying there. He was pale and looked as though he were asleep. She sighed deeply as she approached the bed. "I wish it hadn't come to this."

There was a knock on the door and Mom turned around to find Gram standing there. She entered the room.

"Dr. Marsh just told me what happened. I can't believe this. I go home to shower, and he's alive. I come back, and he isn't." She looked at Dad and paused. "At least he looks peaceful."

Mom gazed at Dad, unable to take her eyes away from him. "I want to believe he's at peace, but after what's happened, I don't know how he can be."

Gram frowned. "What do you mean?"

Mom waved her hand. "It doesn't matter. You wouldn't understand. You never did before."

Gram touched Mom gently from behind. Mom turned to her, and she put her hand on Mom's chin. "Are you alright, darling?"

"I'm sorry that Jeffrey's gone. I cared for him deeply, and my heart breaks for the kids."

"You cared for him, but you didn't love him, did you?"

"I did in a lot of ways. He was a good man, a decent father to my children. He provided for our family and gave me a comfortable life."

Gram took her hand back and nodded. "But he wasn't Damon, was he?"

Mom looked away again. "No, he wasn't."

I was beginning to learn more about my mother than I wanted to know. It was already obvious that she was adept at keeping secrets, and while my parents had difficulties, I didn't realize that she didn't truly love my father. I couldn't help ask myself who Damon was and why he was so important to her.

"I'll leave you alone," Gram said. "I just wanted to tell you how sorry I am." She tried to hug Mom, but Mom moved away. "Has something else happened? You seem, I don't know…strange. Not like yourself at all."

"My husband just died. Forgive me if I'm not Goddamn peppy."

Gram gasped. "Caroline!"

"I'm sorry, Mother. I didn't mean to snap at you."

"I understand. I know you're dealing with a lot. Does Ethan know?"

"He was here and left. I assume he's very upset. You know Ethan when he can't deal with something he escapes…just like me."

"Any word from Shelly yet?"

"Ethan was going to go up to the Wickcliffs to talk to her. I bet that's where he is now. But I haven't heard from him either, and he's not answering his phone. I'm thinking about going to the police. Shelly's got me scared to death."

Gram caressed Mom's arm. "You have enough on your mind as it is without having to worry about Shelly. I'm sure she's fine, Caroline. After all, if Ethan hasn't found her, he'd have called you by now, don't you think?"

Mom nodded. "I suppose you're right. I guess I don't have to do anything right away. If something were wrong, Ethan would call me. I don't want to go to the police any sooner than I have to."

Mom's instincts told her something was wrong. She'd feared that Jeremy had done something to me, but she didn't want to face it. She assumed that I was with Ethan and that I was okay, and she needed to believe that for her own sanity.

"Why don't you let me take you home?" Gram said. "The kids are probably there waiting for us."

"That won't be necessary. I just need to be alone for a little while."

Gram studied her face and knew there was more going on. "I have to say that I'm surprised. You're handling this all too well. Are you sure you don't need anything?"

Mom nodded. "I'm fine."

"You don't have to be strong for my benefit. You can let it out."

Mom started to boil inside. She threw her hands up in the air and clenched her fists. "I told you to leave me alone! What are you waiting for? Are you waiting for me to fall apart? Sob? Turn to you for comfort? Too little, too late, Mother."

Gram opened her mouth in shock and put her hand over her heart. "We all have ways of dealing with grief. If it helps to go off on me, go right ahead. How much longer do you need me to stay here so you can tell me what a horrible mother I am?"

Mom hid her face with her hands. I knew what she was feeling. She was lashing out at Gram because she was overwhelmed by Jeremy's return and at the prospect of having to use her powers again. I could feel my mother's internal pain.

"I'm sorry, Mother. I'm just struggling right now. Go on home. I'll see you later."

"I don't want to leave you like this. Obviously you're in pain."

"I don't want to talk anymore. I just need to be alone."

Gram tried to put her arm around Mom. "I don't think that's such a good idea."

"I've already told you. I'll be fine. Please just go."

Reluctantly, Gram left the room.

Mom went up to Dad's bed, touched his hand and felt how cold it was. "I did love you, you know, even though you may not have been my true love. You knew that. Damon always had my heart but at the same time, you had a piece of it too. I think Jeremy did this to you, and I swear that we're going to make him pay for it." She kissed her fingers and laid them on Dad's lips. "Rest in peace, darling."

For the first time, she let her emotions overtake her, and she wept. Mom had kept so many emotions and secrets inside. I could see from her weeping how much she did love my father, but I also wanted to know more about Damon, and why my mom ended up with my dad instead of being with the man she truly loved.

* * * *

Another night had fallen, and I'd spent another full day trapped in the Wickcliff attic. I'd learned a lot about my family today. I'd always suspected that my brother was gay, but I never knew for sure.

Then there was what I'd learned about my mother's past and that she'd been in love with another man. I was starting to feel overwhelmed by all that I'd learned. I hated being confined to this place. All I could do was stand by and watch as my family suffered.

"Are you alright?" Reed said. "You've been pretty quiet for a while now."

I rubbed my face with my hands. "I don't think I am. I don't know if I can take much more of seeing and feeling everyone's pain. I have enough to worry about as it is." I paused. "I think we may have to use the painting so that I can try to get back to the mortal realm. I know I was reluctant to try it, but I don't have a choice. I don't have any other options, and I can't just stand here and watch my family fall apart. Maybe if I can get closer to them, I can do something." I noticed Reed's morose expression. "What is it?"

"You can't. The painting isn't here."

"What do you mean?"

He pointed behind me, and I turned. The painting wasn't leaning up against the wall where it had been when I pulled him out.

"Where is it?"

He shrugged. "When you were in your trance or whatever you'd call it, Gaul came up here and took it. I tried to talk to him, but he couldn't hear me."

"Terrific. Just terrific. Now what the hell do we do?"

"I was hoping you'd tell me. Did you see anything that would help us?"

"All I've seen is my family suffer. I have to find a way out of here. I can't bear to be in here anymore. I feel as if I'm going to go crazy."

"It's no picnic for me either. I didn't ask to be dragged into this. I didn't ask for my body to be possessed by some psycho and to have my spirit trapped in some purgatory."

"I know that."

"Do you? All I've heard from you is 'me, my.' I've lost a lot too you know. If it weren't for your suicide, I would've never even been summoned to this house. None of this would've even happened."

My face turned red. "Jeremy made me do that, and you know it. Us being trapped here is no more my fault than it is yours. Do you think I've enjoyed seeing all the pain and misery that's going on in the mortal realm? I had to watch my own father's murder."

He bowed his head. "I'm sorry."

I sighed. "We can't turn on each other now. We need one another. There's got to be another way out of here, and if we're going to find it, we have to work together."

He looked up at me. "You didn't answer me. What did you see this time?"

"My mother's a witch."

He rolled his eyes. "There's no such thing."

"Do you believe that? You never thought that an evil spirit could take over your body, did you? There's a lot that happens that we'll never even begin to comprehend."

"Point taken. So what does that mean for us?"

"My mother's friends, Hilda and Gracey, are also witches and the three of them used their powers to fight Jeremy when he was alive. They were friends with his wife, Lucy, and they worked together to bring him down. They know that he's back."

Reed's eyes widened. "Do they know that he's me?"

I shook my head. "They don't know what form he's taken, not yet."

"Well, you have to figure out what else they know. If we can't get out of here, if we can't stop him, our only hope is that they can."

I agreed, but I was feeling drained emotionally. "I'm tired. Connecting with all these people takes a lot out of me."

"You can't stop now. We have to find out what's going on. I want my life back, and you want to find peace. We can't do that if we don't know what's happening."

I nodded. "You're right. I'll try again."

I closed my eyes and took a deep breath. Another picture began to form in my head. I saw Hilda lying on a small, oak twin bed in Gracey's house. She was tossing and turning, thinking about how she could lure Jeremy into the open and figure out the form that he'd taken. This made her think about Lucy as well.

Because I'd never met Lucy, all I knew about her was through Hilda. Although Lucy had been Jeremy's wife, she was nothing like him. She'd been sweet, kind, giving, and warm, the purest of women who had given up her life to end Jeremy's wrath of terror. Lucy had been beautiful both on the inside and outside, and her death had left a hole in Hilda's heart that couldn't be filled.

Hilda accepted that Lucy hadn't been perfect. She had her flaws, but she was also a dynamic, charismatic and loving woman. She'd been the type of person whom people fell in love with the minute they met her. Jeremy had been no exception.

Hilda's mind continued to drift into the past, to the events that led up to Lucy marrying Jeremy. She remembered when Lucy and Jeremy had first met, and how Lucy told her that he had professed his love for her. They hadn't known each other for long at that point, but the way that Lucy's eyes lit up when she talked about him told Hilda that the feeling was mutual.

She tried to warn Lucy that the Wickcliffs weren't what they appeared to be, that they had a history of using manipulation and black magic to get whatever they wanted. Lucy was naive at the time, unaware that Hilda was not only right but that marrying Jeremy would be the beginning of her destruction.

Hilda's eyes became moist as she remembered in vivid detail the night that she'd found out that both Lucy and Jeremy were dead. She'd thought it was the end of a series of events that had changed their lives.

As she thought about the last conversation she had with Lucy on the day of her death, I realized that I not only had the ability to see the present but the past too. I could see Hilda's memories just as clear as I had anything else I'd seen thus far.

On her last day alive, Lucy had been clearly distressed when she met with Hilda. "I've got to get rid of Jeremy tonight. I never wanted to take another life, but I don't have a choice. You were right about him, Hilda, from the very beginning. He's evil personified, and if I stand around and do nothing, his evil will destroy us all."

Hilda touched her arms as if she were going to embrace her. "You can't do it alone. Let us help you. We can come up with another plan together."

Lucy broke free from her. "All previous attempts at getting rid of him using our powers have failed. Gracey almost died, and I don't think her leg will ever be the same again. I'm afraid of what he might do if he's allowed to continue roaming free. He still loves me, and I can use that to my advantage. I have to do this now while I have the opportunity."

"I don't want to see you do this. There has to be another way. Any way you slice it, what you're talking about is murder. Taking a life goes against everything the coven stands for."

"There isn't any other way. Under any other circumstance, I would never even consider this, but getting rid of Jeremy would be a service to humanity. I'm doing it for the greater good."

Hilda met eyes with her. "I don't think you know what you're getting yourself into."

"I can handle Jeremy." Lucy put her hand on Hilda's cheek tenderly and smiled. "If anything happens to me will you promise that my son will be safe?"

"I won't have to because you're going to be fine."

Lucy took Hilda's hand in hers and squeezed it for emphasis. "Please, just promise me."

Hilda nodded. "I promise."

Lucy sealed the promise with a kiss on Hilda's cheek. Although Hilda worried for Lucy's safety after that conversation, she had convinced herself that her friend would prevail. Her instincts didn't tell her that Lucy would die that night. After Lucy's death, she made right on her promise that Lucy's son would never know the Wickcliffs.

Hilda's mind returned to the present, leaving her memories behind. She spoke as if Lucy was in the room with her. "I kept my promise to you. I hope you're at peace knowing that. We kept your son away from the Wickcliffs."

She stopped when she heard the window open. A strong, warm breeze came into the room even though it was chilly outside, and brushed up against her face. She sniffed. The air smelled of Lilacs, Lucy's favorite.

At the foot of the bed, she saw the faint outline of a woman's spirit. It was common for Hilda to see spirits, so this didn't surprise her. Her eyes adjusted to the light that glowed from the spirit, and she was able to make out the figure. It was Lucy who was with her, smiling back at her.

She reached out and called her name, but Lucy was gone as quickly as she'd come. Lucy's spirit had been so close, and now she was gone from her again, just like that.

Unable to sleep, she got out of bed and went to the window. Before she closed it, she looked into the distance at the mansion on the top of the hill, which always loomed over the town like a shadow, and she thought about how much pain the Wickcliffs had caused. She shut the window and looked around the room, hoping for her friend's spirit to appear again.

"We need you, Lucy," Hilda said softly, looking around the room in every corner. "We can't defeat Jeremy alone. You must come back to us. Please."

Chapter 20

I'd previously heard Gaul and Jeremy discussing how they'd planned to return Jeremy's sister, Rachel, to life in my body on this night, and now time was running out. With every second that ticked by, Jeremy was closer to fulfilling his sick plan. I couldn't get Kasey to tell Ethan what I'd shown him, and Hilda and Gracey didn't feel my presence, as surprising as that was. I was beginning to think that there was nothing I could do to stop Jeremy. Hilda, Gracey, and Mom knew that he was alive, but they didn't know whom he inhabited or what he planned to do next.

I saw nothing but darkness as I focused my attention on the Wickcliff mausoleum. Jeremy entered with a wide grin on his face and looked upon my body still lying on the stone tomb where Gaul had laid it down the night before. It was a surreal experience for me seeing my body lying there. It was like looking into a mirror, but without the mirror. It still made me sick that I'd allowed myself to be manipulated by Jeremy into committing suicide.

Jeremy glanced at Gaul, who was standing over my body. "You've done well. Is everything ready?"

Gaul's voice sounded emotionless as always. "We're ready."

Jeremy clasped his hands together, still grinning. "Wonderful. I've waited so long for this." He stroked the hair of my corpse. "Soon my dear Rachel, you'll live and breathe again. You'll recapture the life you lost so unfairly. This time it'll be different. You'll be strong, vibrant, and beautiful. I'm going to give you the life you never had, dear sister."

He peered around the room at the polished marble walls and read off some of the names of the Wickcliff ancestors buried in the tombs. "It won't stop with Rachel. Soon all the Wickcliffs will live and breathe again. Our family will rise from the ashes and have the opportunity to seek revenge on all who have wronged us."

In the center of the mausoleum, he approached the cenotaph, a large stone structure that housed the remains of some more prominent and recent Wickcliff ancestors, including his father, Harold. He touched the cenotaph gently. "You'd be proud of me, Father. I'm alive and will find my son so our legacy can live on." He turned to Gaul. "I wouldn't even know about my son if I hadn't paid off an old gypsy that knew my bitch of a wife." He sighed. "I've been gone for such a long time. My son's a man now."

Gaul stared at him. "How much time do you have to find your son before your spirit dies in this body?"

"I'm not sure, but I have to focus on what I can control now, like bringing Rachel back."

"But you don't even know where he is. What if the gypsy lied to you and you don't even have a son? You've banked your entire existence on finding him. This could be your only opportunity to live again."

"I have no doubt that he exists. I can feel it in my gut. Besides, it would be just like Lucy to spite me by keeping my boy away from me. My only regret is that she's already dead, so I can't make her suffer." He paused and his eyes lit up. "I know exactly what to do. I'll go to Gracey Menze. Lucy confided everything to that old bitch. She'll know where my son is."

"And if she doesn't tell you?"

"I'll make her talk. She'll tell me what I want to know if she values her pathetic life."

Gaul looked back at my corpse. "What do you wish for me to do?"

"You must take care of Rachel when she awakes. Once she's back, and I've found my son, we can concentrate on bringing back the rest of my ancestors one at a time."

Gaul raised an eyebrow. "They'll need to feed on the souls of the living if they're going to be able to survive. It's not going to be easy."

"First things first." Jeremy lit two black candles, one at my corpse's feet, and another by its head. "It's time to begin the ritual."

Jeremy bowed his head and took in a deep breath. He closed his eyes as if he were meditating. I could read his thoughts. He was thinking about the hideous creature that I'd seen in my visions before, the creature that had been his sister. He began to chant.

"In the dark you have slept. In the light, you will rise. Walk again. Breathe again among us as you once did. This body is now yours for the taking. Free your soul from the depths of darkness. Use this vessel as your own."

His eyes sprung open, and the candle's flames reflected in them. The candles flickered wildly, thunder boomed outside, and the mausoleum shook with such force that it made Gaul and him stumble.

He raised his hands above his head. "That's it! Come back to us, Rachel."

He circled his hands over my corpse. Suddenly a dark specter appeared from the tomb below and hovered above the body. It was there for several seconds, its grayish eyes staring down at it. The specter let out a shrill, banshee-like shriek that filled the air. Then I watched helplessly as it entered my corpse and disappeared inside.

My mortal body convulsed violently and then, suddenly, dark purple veins appeared across its white skin. They bulged and receded, and the body's chest rose and fell. With a violent gasp, the eyes opened, but they were no longer my eyes to see with.

Jeremy had been successful. Rachel was alive in my old body and took a deep, gasping breath as if she'd never done so before. He clasped his hands together and grinned with joy and excitement. Gaul stood, staring down at her. I could've sworn that he had a smile on his face.

Although it was supposed to be impossible, Gaul seemed to have feelings for Rachel that were deep and more powerful than any curse the Wickcliffs had put on him.

Jeremy glanced at him. "Happy, Gaul? I suppose you really can't be as you were made not to show any emotion."

"It worked," Gaul said, flatly. "She's come back to us. I mean to you, master."

Thunder shook the walls of the mausoleum once again. "Everything's falling into place." He ran his fingers through Rachel's hair. Her eyes gazed up at him. "I know you don't recognize me dear sister, but it's me, Jeremy. I've returned to life as you have. Oh, how I've longed for this moment, for us to be together again. Can you speak?"

Rachel tried to say something, but nothing came out. She turned her head to Gaul and tears fell from her eyes, moistening her cheeks. She tried to speak again, but it came out as only a whisper.

Jeremy put his finger to her mouth. "No matter, Rachel. You need to rest and get your bearings." He stared back up at Gaul. "It won't be long now, Gaul. Soon the entire family will live again and reclaim what's rightfully ours."

I couldn't stand by and watch this any longer. To see my eyes open, to see my chest heave with breath, with life, was more than I could bear.

I felt as though Jeremy had violated me in the deepest way possible. Not only had he taken my life, but he'd allowed my body to be inhabited by some foreign, dark entity. It didn't matter if Kasey wanted to hear me or not, I had to try to get through to him again, and I wasn't going to stop until I had.

* * * *

By the time Jeremy's ritual was over, the sun was just about to rise to start another day. I saw Kasey in his trailer, now awake with my brother asleep next to him. He was propped up on his elbow looking down at him.

Ethan opened his eyes, pulled his head back, and grinned. "What are you staring at?"

"I'm just watching you sleep," he said, beaming from ear to ear.

Ethan rubbed his eyes. "What time is it?"

"Early, it's morning."

Ethan sprung up. "Morning? It can't be morning. I came over here just before noon. I must've slept an entire day. I have to get home. My mom's probably going berserk."

Kasey put his hands on Ethan's shoulders. "Whoa, tiger. Slow down. You needed the rest."

"You should've woke me up."

"I don't think a nuclear bomb could've woken you up. You were snoring like a freight train."

Ethan hit him on the shoulder. "I was not."

"It's worse than ever."

"I'll have you know I don't snore, Menze."

"Yeah, sure." He poked him. "Maybe I should record it next time and play it back for ya."

Suddenly it seemed as though Ethan relaxed a bit. He began to tickle Kasey playfully. "You're gonna get it!"

Kasey roared with laughter. "Stop! Truce. Truce."

"Not a chance." Ethan continued to tickle him. "Not until you admit that I don't snore."

He could barely speak and put his hands up. "Okay, okay. I give. God, I hate to be tickled."

Ethan stopped. "That's better. I knew I'd get ya to see it my way. That old tickle trick works every time."

"You remembered."

"Of course I did."

Kasey's smile faded, and he suddenly became melancholy.

"What's wrong, Kase? I thought we were having some fun."

"I am having fun. That's why I have to ask you something. Will you stay in Sleepy Meadows?"

Ethan's eyes veered away. "I don't know. I was thinking about staying and working for my dad until he got back on his feet, but now that he's gone, there's no point. Soon there won't even be a business to work at."

He slipped his hand into Ethan's. "If you love me, stay. Stop running. Stop being afraid and embrace what we have."

Ethan leaned his head back on the headboard. "I'm scared, Kase."

"I know it isn't easy, but I believe that your family wouldn't look at you any differently."

"I've already lost my dad. What if I lose the rest of my family too?"

He swallowed and thought about me. "You won't." He got out of the bed and stood up.

"You don't know that."

This was my chance. I focused all my energy on Kasey. I willed him to hear me. I could feel that he was having the same sensation in his head that he'd had the other night at The Hook.

He stumbled backward, hitting the closet door. It was working. I was making contact again. He put both hands on the sides of his head trying to shut out the pain. I was showing him what I'd seen in the mausoleum. He saw my body lying on the tomb. I showed him Rachel, and her distorted and hideous face. He saw her pallid skin, her eyes black and sunken in, and when she opened her mouth, it revealed green rotted teeth. I was trying to show him that this is what Rachel looked like and that she now possessed my body.

"It's not me anymore, Kasey," I said. "The Wickcliffs are responsible for this. You have to tell Ethan that…"

Before I could say another word, Kasey groaned and grabbed both sides of his head. "No!"

He'd shut me out. Somehow he'd found the strength to block out the sound of my voice.

Ethan got out of the bed and grabbed his arms, shaking him. "What's wrong, Kase? Talk to me."

He pushed Ethan away and didn't answer, and then he glanced at Ethan and fell to the floor. Ethan knelt down and grabbed him by the waist, helping him get back in bed.

After a moment, his eyes cleared, and he looked at Ethan. "Where am I?"

"Jesus, Kase, what the hell just happened?"

He caught his breath. "Shelly…" He touched Ethan's face, almost unable to focus his eyes on him.

"What about her?"

"Did you hear from her yet?"

"Reed was at the hospital yesterday when my dad…anyway, he said he'd seen Shelly and that she was going out of town for a few days. She's fine." He groaned. "Oh man. My mom doesn't know that yet. I'm sure she knows about Dad by now, but she probably doesn't know Shelly's been seen." He ran his hands through his blond hair. "I should've gone to her right away. It was selfish of me to go back to the meadows."

"Never mind that now. Are you sure you understood Reed correctly? Shelly left town for a few days?"

"I'm positive. That was a relief, but I still wish she would've told someone where she was going."

He rubbed his head. "That doesn't make sense."

"What doesn't?"

"The whole town knows that she never leaves that house. Are you sure Reed didn't know where she was going?"

Ethan stared at him for a moment. "Are you going to tell me what the hell's wrong with you? First, you act as if you're having a stroke, and then we start playing 20 questions. What's wrong?"

"I can't explain that right now. I'm just relieved to know that Shelly's alright."

Kasey remembered telling Graham about the vision I'd shown him of my death. He'd tried to tell Graham that he thought I was dead, but now Ethan's claim that Reed had seen me had him doubting everything I tried to show him—my death, Rachel inhabiting me, all of it.

Ethan and Kasey believed Jeremy's lie because they had no reason to doubt it. That was going to make it even more difficult for me to get Kasey to trust his instincts.

"Maybe you should see a doctor," Ethan said. "I'm worried about you. I just got you back, and I'll be damned if I lose you again."

"You won't." Kasey forced a smile. "I'm okay. I haven't been feeling well, and I got a little lightheaded when I stood up, that's all. I haven't spent the kind of energy I did yesterday in a while. It'll take a while to recover." He sat up and touched Ethan's face. "Maybe you should go see your family now. They're going to need you."

Ethan nodded. "I have to face my mom and Gram. We have a lot of arrangements to make." He touched Kasey's forehead. "Are you sure you're okay? You feel kinda warm."

Kasey waved his hand and smiled. "I'll be fine. Go see your family. I'll catch up with you later."

Once dressed, Ethan kissed Kasey and walked out the door. After he left, Kasey laid his head on his pillow and sighed. While he believed Jeremy's lie, I could feel that a part of him still wanted to believe that what I'd shown him was real. He wanted to believe that I was okay, but there was a part of him that knew otherwise. I just had to get him to trust that part of himself.

* * * *

I followed Ethan home. As much as I wanted to try to get through to Kasey and to make him understand, it was obvious that every time I tried to make contact with him, it took a physical toll on him. I needed to give him a break. I couldn't jeopardize his health. Besides, there was nothing that he could do about Rachel immediately.

Ethan arrived home and walked into Mom's kitchen. He found Gram cooking breakfast and Mom sitting at the table. Both of them stared at him, noticing that he had the same clothes on that he'd worn the day before.

Mom stood up and approached him. "Where were you yesterday and last night?" she asked, anger welling up in her. "Dr. Marsh said he'd talked to you after your father died. How could you just disappear like that?"

"I needed some time alone," Ethan said. "I'm sure you can understand that."

"You should've called us to let us know where you were. You were supposed to go up to the Wickcliffs to talk to your sister. When I didn't hear from either of you, I got scared, and I've asked Graham to come over this morning."

"I'm sorry. I didn't mean to scare you. I just couldn't stay at the hospital anymore, and I didn't see you. I had to get out of there."

Gram stood at the stove scrambling eggs. "I'm surprised at you, Ethan. Your mother could've used your support last night."

He dropped his shoulders and scoffed. "I don't believe this."

Mom sighed and put up her hand. "I can handle this, Mother."

Gram finished the eggs and turned the burner off. "I'm just saying. It's bad enough that Shelly's gone, and then you took off."

"I didn't come back here to be attacked. I'm fine, by the way. Thanks for asking. Dad's death didn't affect me at all."

Gram approached him and put her hand on his shoulder. "I'm sorry, darling. I know you have to be in pain. It's just that you scared us when you disappeared."

Mom hugged him and softened her tone. "I'm sorry too. It's just that you could've called. Especially since you knew that we're so concerned about Shelly."

He broke the embrace. "If you would've given me a chance, I would've told you that Shelly's fine."

Mom's eyes broadened. "You know where she is?"

"Not exactly," he said, sitting down at the table. "I ran into Reed at the hospital yesterday. He'd been up at the Wickcliffs and said he saw her. Shelly told him she needed to get away. I'm sorry. I should've told you right away. After what happened to Dad, I just wasn't thinking straight."

"But she hasn't called," Mom said, lowering her eyebrows. "We've left her numerous messages. She doesn't even know about your father yet. Why wouldn't she call us back?"

"And she hasn't called to check on Freddy," Gram said. "We don't see her much anymore, but at least she calls to check in on him."

Ethan pulled out his phone. "Let me try again. You're right. She at least should have told Reed where she was going." He let the phone go to voicemail and put it away. "She's still not answering." He thought about the conversation he had with me just a few days before he came back. He remembered how worried he'd been that my sanity was delicate.

"What is it, Ethan?" Mom put her hand on his shoulder noticing that his mind had wandered. "Something's bothering you."

"It's stupid. We think Shelly's fine, but before we lost Dad, he was convinced that she was in danger."

Gram shot a concerned look at him and then at Mom. "What are you talking about?"

Mom's eyes drifted away and then she looked at Ethan again. "Your father was on a lot of medication, and he was confused."

"I didn't believe you when you tried pulling that crap on me before," he said, "and I don't believe it now. I saw the look on your face when Dad said Jeremy was coming back."

"Jeremy Wickcliff?" Gram said, her face going pale. "Will someone tell me what in heaven's name is going on here?"

"Nothing, Mother," Mom said. "Jeffrey was confused as I said."

"I don't think so," he said. "Dad was so adamant about what Shelly said. Now she just vanishes, and no one sees her but Reed? Something doesn't add up."

Mom put her hand up. "Stop it, Ethan. Stop it right now. Shelly's fine. She'll call."

Ethan grabbed her arm. "Mom, I know that you're scared, but if we're going to find out where Shelly is, you have to start being honest with us."

That's it, Ethan. You know Mom's hiding something. There's a lot more to her than you think. You have to keep pushing her to tell the truth. Don't let up on her.

Mom yanked her arm away. "I resent my own son calling me a liar."

Ethan turned to Gram. "How often does she call to check on Freddy?"

"Every few days," Gram said. "It's odd that she hasn't called. Even if she did go away, she'd at least want to know her little boy's safe."

"At least he is safe," Mom said. "That's something. I'm glad that she trusted him with us so that he doesn't have to grow up in that prison. We have to get her out of there too. Rory's been dead for years. There's no reason for her to stay in that house. It's about time we bring her home so that she and her son can be together."

"She won't leave," Gram said. "You know that."

"We can't argue about that now," Mom said. "Things are different now."

He tilted his head. "What do you mean? You do know more than you're saying, don't you?"

"I don't know what I meant." She looked away from him.

"I don't care what that Withers boy says," Gram said. "I told her numerous times in my messages that it was an emergency. She wouldn't leave town without telling us where she was going. What if we needed to find her because of Freddy? His story doesn't make sense, and if it doesn't make sense, it isn't true."

There was a knock on the door. Mom went to it and opened it to find Graham standing on the porch.

He removed his hat. "Good morning, Carol. My deputy tells me that you wanted to see me. What can I do for you?"

Mom stepped aside. "Won't you come in?"

Graham entered the house, and Mom shut the door after him.

"How are you folks holding up?"

"We're doing fine, considering," Mom said, walking back to the kitchen. Graham followed her and saw Ethan standing there.

"Hello, Ethan. It's nice to see you again. I'm sorry it has to be under these circumstances."

He shook Graham's hand. "It's good to see you too, Sheriff."

"Your father's going to be missed. He was a good man."

"Thank you."

Graham turned to Mom. "So tell me, why did you want to see me?"

"We haven't heard from Shelly in a few days, and she isn't returning any of our calls. Reed told Ethan that he saw her and she was fine and needed to get away. She didn't say where she was going, and I'm starting to think that something happened after she left."

Graham raised an eyebrow. "Reed says he saw her? When I saw him at the hospital yesterday, he didn't say anything about it. I guess I don't have as much reason to be concerned."

"What do you mean?" Mom said. "Did you know we thought she was missing?"

Graham nodded. "I wasn't going to bring this up because it hasn't been too long, and I figured you had enough to deal with, but Kasey came to see me the night before last. He said he was concerned about Shelly because she hadn't returned your phone calls. He wanted me to go up to the Wickcliffs and check on her."

"He didn't say anything to me," Ethan said. He glanced at Mom, realizing he'd given away his whereabouts.

Mom turned to him. "You were with Kasey?"

"We ran into one another." Ethan shifted his attention back to Graham. "Did you go up to the Wickcliffs?"

Graham nodded. "She wasn't home. Her car was gone. Now I know why. What I can't figure out is why her purse was still in her room. If she were going away, I'd think that she'd need her ID and money."

Mom scratched her head. "Her purse was there, but her car was gone?" Her face whitened.

"Correct. I'm not trying to alarm you. I'm just giving you the facts."

"I went up there to tell Shelly about Jeffrey's attack," Gram said. "The maid said that she hadn't seen her. Shelly wouldn't just go without telling the staff that she wasn't going to be back for a while. I'm getting worried."

"I talked with Greta too," Graham said. "I got the same story. When did you go there, Edith?"

"It was before midnight. We were at the hospital. We'd been

worried because she hadn't picked up her phone all afternoon and into the evening."

Graham rubbed his chin. "I was up there afterwards. I woke Greta and Irma right up out of a sound sleep. Shelly wasn't accounted for. I agree that she at least should be returning your calls."

"I don't like this at all," Gram said. "Something's fishy, and I think we need to file a missing person's report."

"I'll talk to my son to try to get some more details," Graham said. "Technically she's not missing if someone's seen her. Just because you don't know where she went, doesn't mean that she's missing. I agree with Ethan though. There's a slight possibility that maybe something happened between the time Reed saw her and now. I'll tell you what I'll do. If you don't hear from her within 24 hours, give me a call, and I'll launch an investigation."

Mom sat down at the table. "I couldn't bear it if something's happened to Shelly too."

"Let's not get ahead of ourselves," Graham said. "Hopefully you'll hear from her before the 24 hours is up, and it'll be a non-issue."

He left the house and walked to his car. Ethan followed him and stopped him before he got into his car. "Sheriff, wait up, I need to talk to you about something else." He looked back at the house and then lowered his voice. "It's about something my dad said to me before he died."

"What did he say?"

"He said he was going up to the Wickcliffs the day he had his heart attack because Shelly called him. He said she was sobbing uncontrollably on the phone and that she said she heard voices."

Graham swallowed, remembering what Irma had told him about what I'd said to her about hearing voices. He kept his composure, but all he thought about was what Kasey had told him about having seen Reed and Pit carrying what looked like a body through the cemetery.

He was starting to believe there was something seriously wrong.

Chapter 21

"Voices?" Graham said, not letting on what he knew.

Ethan nodded. "He was really worried about her and was convinced she was in trouble."

"Why would he say that?"

Ethan shook his head. "I don't know."

Graham narrowed his eyes. "You know she hasn't been the same since Rory died, Ethan, and since you left. That was a mess."

"I'd rather not talk about that if it's all the same to you."

"All I'm saying is that it makes sense for your father to think she sounded fragile. It's not every day when a woman witnesses her husband shoot himself."

Ethan knew that wasn't what happened. "I know. She's never been the same."

"Why did you come back here, Ethan? It couldn't be because of your father's condition. From what I understand from talking to Kasey, you were here before you even heard about his heart attack."

"I thought it was time to come back. Honestly, I've been worried about Shelly. I'm glad that I'm here now for my family."

"I'm sure they are too." Graham gave him a closed smile and put his hand on Ethan's shoulder. "Thanks for telling me, Ethan, but I'm sure Shelly's alright. I'm sure you'll hear from her soon."

Graham didn't realize that Ethan was still hiding the fact that he suspected that our mother was hiding something. Her reaction to Dad's panic appeared to be genuine fear, but then she so adamantly denied that she'd believed him at all. He wanted to save Mom from any additional questioning, fearing that she couldn't handle it, and he had no proof that she was hiding anything. Telling the police he thought our mother was lying wouldn't accomplish anything, and he knew it.

Ethan gave him a nod. "I hope you're right." He stepped back from Graham and watched him get into his car and pull out of the driveway, not exactly sure what he believed.

Graham wasn't sure either. I could see the doubt in his eyes when he was talking to Ethan. Kasey had said he thought I was dead. He didn't want to believe that for obvious reasons, but also because Reed had said he'd seen me and said I was fine. If he believed that I was dead, it could mean that his son was lying or somehow involved, and he couldn't accept that.

* * * *

I didn't know why, but after I watched Graham drive down the road, my thoughts gravitated back to Rebecca. I didn't realize what was so relevant about her in relation to my situation, but I was about to find out.

She was sitting in the Golden Crescent Diner, almost falling asleep at the counter. She looked as though she hadn't slept. She was thinking about Ethan. She'd heard through the grapevine about Dad's passing. In a small town like Sleepy Meadows, the word spread like wildfire. She was thinking about going to see him but thought better of it. She felt as though he needed time with his family. Instead, she just left him a message telling him to call her if he needed anything.

I could feel her loneliness as I concentrated on her. Although she'd ended things with Pit and was relieved, she didn't feel any less lonely. All she felt like was a failure for having a marriage that fell apart. She glanced upon the booth she'd shared with the mysterious stranger, Jason, and wondered if she'd see him again. As if it were fate, her thoughts were disrupted by the sound of his voice.

"Is this seat taken?"

She smiled widely when she saw him standing there. "Not at all."

"Fancy seeing you here again."

"I didn't feel like staying home."

"Well, this is the place to get a tasty meal cheap. I need to pinch my pennies. I'm glad I ran into you. I wanted to thank you again for talking with your friend and getting me a room at the inn. He's going to let me do some repairs there in exchange for the room."

"I'm glad it worked out for you. No need to thank me."

"It was nice to sleep on a comfortable bed for a change. You mind if I sit down? I was able to shower this morning, so I promise I smell better."

She motioned to the seat next to her. "Sit, please."

He did, but he could tell that something was wrong. "You okay, Becca? You seem...sad."

She nodded. "Remember my friend Ethan I told you about? His father died."

He sat back and exhaled. "I'm sorry to hear that."

"You're worried about your chances of getting a job now, aren't you?"

His face turned red. "Is it that obvious? You must think I'm selfish."

She took a sip of coffee and set it down. "Not at all. We all have to make a living. I still plan to talk to Ethan. This just delays it a bit. I would imagine that he's going to be the one making all the business decisions from here on out."

"I can't believe you'd do that for me. We hardly know one another."

She waved her hand. "It's no big deal. Don't think twice about it." She looked into his green eyes, and he smiled back at her, which was infectious and made her happy for a change. Her attraction to him made her feel alive again.

He picked up a menu and glanced down at it.

"You're not going to order a hamburger again, are you?" she asked.

He laughed. "Very funny. Would it kill you if I did?"

"I'm not sure. I do feel sick to my stomach, so watching you eat raw meat might just make me lose it."

He perused the menu quickly and pointed. "So I guess the liver and onions are out, huh?"

She cringed, and they both laughed. She felt an intense physical attraction growing between them and thought fleetingly about making love to him. She wondered how she could want someone she barely knew much about.

As I studied Jason's face, I could see why Rebecca found him attractive. He reminded me a lot of Jeremy, handsome, but his looks masked his true intentions. Rebecca was only seeing Jason's looks and winning smile, just as Lucy had with Jeremy in the beginning. If Jason was Jeremy's son, I hoped that Rebecca wasn't going down the same path that Lucy had. I still wasn't sure if he was Jeremy's son or not. Although he resembled Jeremy more than Kasey, from what I'd heard from Hilda and Gracey's conversation, Kasey appeared to be the Wickcliff heir.

I didn't want to believe that could be Kasey's destiny. I wasn't sure what to believe anymore. Being able to see and hear things was more of a curse than anything. I was left with more questions than answers, and I needed to figure out the truth if I was going to find a way to stop Jeremy.

* * * *

I'd spent the remainder of the day focused on my family. I watched as my mom and Ethan made funeral arrangements for my father. I wondered where he was, and if I ever would see him again. I'd gathered that as good of a person as he was, that he'd gone on to heaven or another realm, and I hoped that I'd be able to get out of the spirit realm someday so we could be together again.

Reed and I talked, and I filled him in on what else I'd learned during my connections to the mortal realm. I was tired, so I took a break from trying to make contact with anyone. Kasey had shut me out because he was afraid of his visions and because he'd believed Jeremy's lie about my going away. No one else could see or hear me. Frustrated and exhausted, I decided to let my spirit rest.

The next day was my father's wake, and I wanted to be there with my family, at least in spirit. As I focused my energy on making contact with my loved ones, I saw Mom and Ethan standing next to Dad's casket.

"He just looks so peaceful doesn't he, Ethan?" Mom said. "The past few months have been so hard for him. He struggled with Shelly's depression, and he blamed himself. I wasn't sure before, but I feel like he's finally at peace. It's comforting in a way."

"I'd rather have him here," Ethan said, putting his hand on the casket uncomfortably. "This just feels so wrong."

She rubbed his arm tenderly. "I'm glad you came back and were here to say goodbye. All he ever talked about was how much he missed you and how much he wanted you to come home. You made one of his final wishes come true." She sighed. "I know we haven't always seen eye-to-eye, even now, but I'm glad you're here too, not just because you were here for your father, but because you're here with me."

He wiped a tear from his eye and gazed at her. "I should've been here for him all along, for both of you."

His pain was immense, and it seemed to be growing. He felt guilty because he hadn't been there for either one of our parents for the past five years. He knew that he couldn't get the time he'd lost with Dad back, and it was killing him. I wished that I could've told him I felt the same way. Although I never left Sleepy Meadows, as Jeremy caused my mental state to decline, I kept my distance from my family. I wanted them to remember me the way I was before. Now it was too late.

His hands followed along the ridge of the casket and tears spilled down his cheeks. "I'm sorry, Dad." He started to walk away and saw Rebecca walk in.

Mom saw her too. "Why don't you go ahead and talk to her?"

He wiped his cheeks. "Are you sure you don't want me to stay here with you?"

"I'm okay. You go ahead."

He walked over to the other side of the room where Rebecca stood. She touched his arm. "Do you need another hug?"

He smiled through the tears as they embraced. "I can never get enough of those, especially if they come from you."

She separated from him, although she didn't want to. "I'm so sorry. If there's anything I can do…"

"Just you being here's enough. I appreciate it."

She gave a nod towards the door. "It looks like someone else thought you could use a shoulder."

He turned and saw Kasey in the doorway.

She nudged him and gave him a wink. "Are you just going to stand there looking like a dork or are you going to go to him? I know you want to."

He swallowed. "What's the wink for?"

"Kasey came here to comfort you. You need to let him or else you're both going to regret it."

By the look in her eye, he knew she knew about him and Kasey. He smiled at her and then walked up to greet Kasey. "You came."

"Of course I did." He put his hand on Ethan's shoulder and squeezed gently. "I needed to make sure you were alright. How are you holdin' up?"

"Honestly? Not so good."

Kasey rubbed Ethan's arm. "It kills me to see you like this. Is there anything I can do?"

Ethan shuffled uncomfortably and thought about sharing Kasey's bed. "I don't know if there's anything anyone can do."

Mom came up behind them. "Kasey, can I speak to you for a moment?"

Kasey turned to face her. "Sure."

She pulled him aside. "I've spoken with Sheriff Withers, and he said you told him about us not being able to get in touch with Shelly and that you were worried, so you went up to the Wickcliffs to try to find her. Is that true?"

He nodded. "Yes, ma'am."

"Why didn't you tell us?"

"The sheriff told me to stay out of it. He said he'd follow up on it and that I should go home."

"Thank you for your concern, Kasey. We appreciate it. Graham said that it looked like Shelly left town in a hurry, without her purse and money. We still haven't heard from her. I've had to file a missing person's report."

"I hope I didn't add to your concer. I didn't mean to. I'm dreadfully sorry for what you're going through, Mrs. Hawkins. My mom sends her condolences and wishes she could be here."

Mom didn't acknowledge that she had just seen Gracey or everything they'd talked about. "I understand. Give Gracey my thanks."

When Kasey approached my brother again, Ethan looked puzzled. "Why didn't you say anything to me about going to the Wickcliffs to try to find my sister?"

"I was going to, but after everything that happened with your dad, I didn't want you to worry about Shelly too."

"Well I am worried, and I have been. We still don't know where she is."

"I'm right behind you," a female voice said.

Chapter 22

Ethan whipped around with his mouth agape and saw Rachel standing in the doorway. Of course, he thought it was me.

Half of the room gasped. The rest of them didn't realize that I'd been missing. It's surreal watching yourself walk into a room. No one standing there, gazing upon Rachel in the doorway, had any inkling that it wasn't me. She looked stunning in a tight black dress with her black hair pulled up in a bun away from her face setting off what had been my brilliant blue eyes.

Ethan walked up to her. "Where the hell have you been, Shelly?"

"Hello, Ethan," she said, smiling. "It's good to see you too."

He grabbed her by the arms and pulled her aside, trying not to make a scene. "We've been worried sick. What the hell's wrong with you? Why haven't you returned any of our calls?"

She yanked her arm away and rubbed it. "Don't grab me like that. You're way too rough. Is that any way to greet your sister after all this time?"

He put his hands up and softened his voice. "I'm sorry. I didn't mean to hurt you."

She rubbed her arm again. "I can explain everything. But first, I need to take care of something."

She brushed past him and approached Dad's coffin. She put on a brilliant show and stood in silence by his coffin, her head bowed down, knowing people were watching her. Before returning to my family, she wiped the fake tears from her eyes.

She approached Mom. "I'm so sorry, Mom."

Mom's brow was furrowed, and she narrowed inquisitive eyes at her. If anyone would know that Rachel wasn't me, it would've been my mother. I'd seen her little demonstration at Gracey's house, and it didn't matter that she hadn't used the; she still had powers. She wasn't any more aware of Rachel's identity than anyone else was.

Mom put her hand on her hip. "Where have you been?"

"Ethan already asked that. I went to Misty Lake to clear my head. You remember. It's where Rory and I used to go together. It's where we spent our honeymoon."

"Of course I remember."

"Well, then you must remember it's also the anniversary of his death. Anyway, I just got back a little while ago. I had no idea that Daddy was so sick. I wish to God that I'd been here."

Mom put her hand over her mouth and then hugged her. Tears streamed down her face. "Darling, we were all so worried. I even talked to the police."

Rachel broke the embrace. "I went to our cabin because I needed to feel close to him again. There isn't cell service up there, or I would've called you back. I just got all your messages including the one about the service today. I rushed right over."

Ethan sighed. I could tell that he was relieved thinking that I was alright after all. "You should've told someone where you were going. Reed knew you were going, but he didn't know where. We thought that something terrible happened to you."

"I'm sorry. What more can I say? Today's a day to remember our father. We need to focus on that."

"That isn't good enough, Shelly. We thought you were hurt or worse. You're so nonchalant about it all."

She threw her hands up. "I said I was sorry. What do you want me to do, open a vein? You're the one that hasn't been here for Dad for five years. I take off for a few days, and you make a federal case of it?"

Ethan huffed. "Hey, I—"

Mom put her hand up. "Stop it right now, both of you."

"I'm sorry, Ethan," Rachel said. "You know I didn't mean that."

He shook his head. "Here we are fighting at our father's wake. We're being ridiculous. What am I going to do with you? Come here." He embraced her, but she tensed up. "Are you okay?"

She stepped back and feigned a smile. "I'm fine. I'm just upset."

A few minutes after exchanging pleasantries with Mom, Gram, and other guests, Ethan and Rachel were left alone together.

"Maybe you should come over to the house after this for a little while," Ethan said. "Mom could use both of us right now."

"I'll be there."

"I think you need to spend some time with Freddy too. He misses you."

"And I him. You know, I've been thinking of talking to Mom about Freddy coming home with me at some point. With everything that's happened, she'll probably be relieved."

My heart sank. The thought of my son in the mansion alone with Rachel and Jeremy sickened me. I could only hope that Mom would refuse to let Rachel take him.

He raised an eyebrow. "When I talked to you last week, you admitted that you didn't think you could care for him. You called yourself unstable. You said he'd be better off with Mom and Dad."

"I know what I said. I was just having a terrible time last week. I didn't mean that. Besides, with Dad gone, looking after Freddy might be too much for Mom to handle alone. He's my son and my responsibility."

He narrowed his eyes. My brother wasn't stupid. He knew something wasn't right. "Shelly, you cried about it for an hour on the phone."

She shrugged. "What can I say? The time away helped me clear my head. I'm in a much better place now. It's been six months since I've had my son, and I'm ready for him to come home."

She turned her back and began to walk away, but he stepped in front of her. "I wasn't about to mention this in front of anyone, but Dad said you called him the day that he had his heart attack, and you were hysterical. He thought something terrible had happened to you, and that Jeremy Wickcliff had something to do with it. That doesn't sound to me like you've been doing any better at all. Why would you call him and then take off to Misty Lake when you knew that he was on his way to talk to you?"

She shook her head. "That's insane. I don't know what you're talking about. Jeremy's dead. Everyone in Sleepy Meadows knows that. Sometimes I think that it was Dad who had the mental problems."

"He seemed pretty sane to me. He said you called, and you were sobbing uncontrollably. Is that what happened or not?"

Her face tightened, and she looked straight at him. "I never talked to Dad."

He raised his eyebrows. "You're sure about that?"

"Positive." She glanced past him into the crowd, then back at him with an irritated expression. "I'm tired of the third degree and how you've been treating me today. You seem almost insensitive to the fact that I've also lost my father." She sighed heavily. "We'd better start going around and thanking people for coming. I don't want to talk about this again."

* * * *

Rachel stepped away from Ethan and stopped in her tracks when she bumped into Kasey a few feet away.

He stared at her as if he'd seen a ghost. "You're here. If I didn't see it for myself, I wouldn't believe it."

"Why wouldn't I be here? This is my father's wake." She folded her arms. "Why are you staring at me?"

"I was worried about you. I went to the police to try and find you."

"Well, you shouldn't have done that. It was none of your business, and I explained to all of you where I was."

She started to walk away from him, but he pulled on her arm. She whipped around glaring at him with disgust and annoyance. "Why does everyone here think they can manhandle me? I'm growing tired of it really fast." She glared at his hand. "Let go."

He felt her cold skin. The image of the grotesque woman from the vision I'd shown him in his trailer flashed in front of his face again. He saw Rachel for whom she was. He narrowed one eye at her. "It's you. You're what I saw in my vision."

She jerked her arm from his grasp. "I beg your pardon?"

He swallowed hard and shook his head. "You're not Shelly. Who and what are you?"

"That's it, Kasey," I said. *"You know that lying manipulative bitch isn't me. You have to tell someone."*

Rachel laughed it off, but I could tell that he'd gotten to her. She glanced around the room. It appeared that the only one who was within earshot was Ethan, but she didn't think he'd heard what Kasey had said. She exhaled sharply.

"I have no idea what you're talking about. Please, I have friends here that have known my father his whole life, and I need to speak with them. Excuse me." Rachel dashed away leaving him standing there alone and bewildered.

Kasey had to know now that everything I'd shown him was real. He knew Rachel wasn't me and soon everyone else would know it too.

* * * *

She didn't know it, but Ethan heard what Kasey had said and wondered what he meant. His immediate thought was how I could've changed so much. Rachel had sauntered into the funeral parlor with a confidence and arrogance he'd never seen in me before. He'd known me as the despondent, broken woman of the recent past.

He wondered why Kasey would say what he said and more importantly, what had changed within me in the past week to make me seem so different? For the first time since my death, I was hopeful. I finally had an ally in Kasey, and I was going to take full advantage of it.

* * * *

Hours later, I watched Rachel prepare to leave the funeral home. She may have thought that she'd fooled all my loved ones, but Kasey knew better, and Ethan was suspicious too. I felt sorry for Kasey. I'd shown him things because I'd known that he could see and hear me, but I'd failed to realize the situation I put him in. He couldn't tell anyone. He was afraid that no one would believe him, especially now that someone looking and sounding like me had shown up. He also feared his visions would cost him his sobriety as they had before. I loved him, and I didn't want to put him through this, but I had no one else to turn to.

I watched as he talked to Rebecca, who was also convinced that there was something strange about me. She'd told him she'd attributed my behavior to the fact that I'd lost my father, but he knew better.

He walked away, and I was going to follow him, but I'd noticed that Pit was exchanging words with Rachel before she left, and he seemed frightened. He was the only person in attendance that knew who she truly was.

Rebecca decided to go up to him, and I decided to keep my attention on her. Maybe I'd learn something. She approached him. His back was to her, and she tapped him on the shoulder. He flinched and whipped around.

"You look like you've seen a ghost, Pit."

"Don't do that!"

She took a step backward. "What's wrong with you?"

"I don't like looking at dead people, okay?"

"That's a horrible thing to say about Ethan's father."

"I didn't mean him." Pit looked away.

Rebecca put her hands on her hips. "You aren't making much sense lately, you know that? And what's got you so jumpy? I thought you'd be gone by now after I caught you packing the other night. I guess that was just wishful thinking on my part."

He glared at her. "You don't care about me or why I'm here. There was a change of plans, and I'm stickin' around. You're probably just upset because you were going to start screwing half the town the minute I had my back turned."

Rebecca laughed. "I don't need a man to satisfy that need. After all, I've gone this long without being satisfied."

"I don't have the time or the patience for you right now. If you aren't going to come back, I want your stuff out of my house by the end of the week, or it goes in the street where it belongs."

"I need more time than that. I haven't been gone that long, and if my parents were to know that our marriage was over, they wouldn't even let me stay there at all. You know how they feel about divorce. I have to find somewhere more permanent."

He shrugged. "Oh well. You left me remember? You aren't my problem anymore."

Pit pushed his way past her, but she grabbed his arm and made him face her again. She studied his face and saw how frightened he'd become. "You can act like an ass as much as you want to. I know it comes as second nature to you, but I always know when you're hiding something. Whatever it is you've done, whatever trouble you've gotten yourself into, don't expect me to come bailing you out this time."

Pit glared at her, and she let go of his arm. She turned around to see

Jason standing there. Her expression softened. "What are you doing here?"

"You told me about the wake, remember? I thought I'd check in. I wanted to see you." Jason's eyes shifted to Pit.

Pit scowled at him and then at Rebecca. "So you're proving my point. I knew you just couldn't wait to start screwing around on me. Did you have to bring your latest conquest to a funeral? That's sick."

She ignored him. As happy as she was to see Jason, I could tell that she was wondering if he'd come just to ask Ethan about a job.

"This isn't about the job or anything," Jason said, almost reading her mind. "I was just hoping to see you."

Pit stepped in front of him. "Who are you?"

Jason stuck his hand out. "My name's Jason Beckett."

Pit didn't shake it and made a face at Rebecca. "You don't have to flaunt your boy toy in my face. Is that what gets you off?"

"It's not any of your business. But, if you must know, I met him down by the docks the other night when you and I had a fight. He's new in town, and we're just friends."

"So you're meeting strange men down by the docks now? He's more than a friend, and I know it. Guys are after one thing. Can you at least try to be discreet about who you're screwing?"

Jason stepped forward. "Watch what you say to the lady."

Pit got in his face. "Or what?"

Jason pushed him backward. "I don't want any trouble here. It was an accidental meeting. Why don't you just apologize to Becca?"

"Oh, so it's Becca now?" Pit smirked and then turned to her. "No more meeting down by the docks. If you insist on being a whore, you can at least do it in private."

Jason groaned. "Alright, that's it. You need to treat her with some respect, and if you don't know how, I'll just have to show you."

People at the funeral home started staring at them, which prompted Rebecca to put her arms between them. "Enough, alright?" She glared at Pit. "Just leave. No one wants you here. You barely even knew Mr. Hawkins. If you came here just to spy on me, take a good look at me now because you won't be seeing me again."

Pit grunted and stepped back, eyeing Jason. "If you can get those legs open, she's all yours, buddy. But be careful, you'll probably have to pry them open and clear out the cobwebs first." He huffed like a child, whipped around, and stormed out the front doors.

Jason turned to her and raised an eyebrow. "That's your husband? Not exactly what I expected."

She nodded. "Me either. If I'd known then what I know now, my whole life could've been different. He won't be my husband for long. It's time I rectify that mistake."

He touched her arm. "Are you alright? He said some pretty cruel things."

She waved her hand. "That's nothing compared to what he normally says. I'm used to it."

"You shouldn't have to be used to it. He should treat you with the respect you deserve."

She glanced around the room and saw Ethan and Kasey looking over at her with concerned expressions. She waved her hand showing them that everything was alright, smiled and turned back to Jason.

Jason saw them. "Who are they?"

"The blond man's Ethan Hawkins. He's the one I told you about. The brown-haired one's his best friend, Kasey. Kasey lives here in Sleepy Meadows. We all grew up together."

Jason looked over at them again. He gave them a slight wave and smiled. They nodded and went back to talking.

Rebecca took his arm. "Let's get out of here. I could use some fresh air."

They stepped outside into the courtyard and found a bench to sit on. Jason put his hand on her knee. "You look lovely today. I've missed talking to you. I know we just saw each other, but to me it feels like such a long time ago."

"I feel the same way." She blushed, noticing that he wasn't removing his hand. His green eyes sparkled in the sunlight, and she was now feeling a passion she thought she never would again. She wanted him, and it was becoming harder and harder for her to hide it.

"I feel bad. I didn't mean to cause you any problems by coming here. Who comes to a stranger's wake just to see a woman he barely knows? You must think I'm totally lame."

Midnight's Edge, The Secrets of Sleepy Meadows

She smiled and put her hand on his. "Not at all. In fact, I think it's sweet that you went through the trouble so that we could see each other."

They were silent for a moment, and then he broke it. "Who was the dark-haired, young woman I saw leaving when I came in?"

"That was Shelly Wickcliff. She's Ethan's younger sister. She'd been missing for the last few days. No one knew where she was. She just turned up today like nothing happened. She seems so different. I can't quite explain the change, and you wouldn't understand anyway having never met her."

Jason remembered the name from the old man who picked him up on the side of the road. He'd accused him of being a Wickcliff, and he had denied it. He wasn't sure who he was, and I could feel he was telling the man the truth when he said he'd never heard the name. There was a reason why the name had stuck with him.

I felt as though there was a part of him that wanted to believe he could be a part of the Wickcliff family so that he'd have an identity for the first time in his life. He was almost sure it was a long shot, but I wasn't.

"Ethan's sister's a Wickcliff?" he asked.

"She was married to Rory, a distinguished, kind gentleman from Europe, a distant nephew of Irma, the old woman who owns the mansion now."

"Was? What happened to him? I didn't see him there with her."

"He died years ago. Ethan and Shelly were with him when he shot himself."

"Wow, that's horrible."

"Shelly's never been the same since the suicide. They have a little boy named Freddy who stays with the Hawkinses most of the time. My teenage sister, Brynn, babysits for him often. That's what I guess has got me confused. I haven't seen Shelly present herself so well since Rory died, not that I've seen her that often. I suppose her trip to the lake did her a world of good."

Jason's eyes drifted away. She patted his knee. "Penny for your thoughts?"

He glanced back at her with a smile. "Sorry, I didn't mean to let my mind wander."

"Was it something I said?"

He put his arm around her and kissed her gently on the lips. She closed her eyes, not wanting him to stop. They stopped kissing when they heard Pit's voice behind them.

"What the hell are you doing?"

Rebecca and Jason turned. They stood up and faced him.

"Not again," Jason said. "I thought you left."

Rebecca put her hands on her hips. "Pit, leave us alone. I'm not going to tell you again."

Mom heard the commotion and came outside. She'd witnessed his outburst inside and grabbed Pit's arm. "You're leaving."

Pit jerked his arm back. "Stay out of this, Mrs. Hawkins."

She grabbed his arm even harder. "You won't create a scene here, Pit Bowen. Leave right now!"

Mom glared at Rebecca and Jason as Pit stormed back inside. She followed him inside.

"I have to go," Rebecca said. "He's throwing a temper tantrum like a child. It's the last thing Ethan or Mrs. Hawkins need today."

Jason nodded. "I understand. I shouldn't have come here. When will I see you again?"

"How about tomorrow?"

"Sounds wonderful."

She took his hand. "How 'bout I meet you at the docks around noon? I have a special place I'd like to show you."

He gave her a wink and kissed her on the cheek. She walked towards the door of the funeral home and turned back to wave to him before she entered, finding that he had already left.

Rebecca wasn't the only one who felt like there was an exceptional amount of mystery surrounding this stranger. I did too. He'd come to town the night of my death, seeking answers about where it was he'd come from. The way he reacted to the name Wickcliff didn't sit right with me. He hadn't known anything about his family, just as Kasey hadn't, but it was clear that Jeremy's son couldn't be anyone other than the two of them, but which one was it?

* * * *

I took a moment in the spirit realm after seeing Rebecca and explained what I'd seen to Reed.

"So now what do we do?" he asked. "Kasey knows what happened to you and knows that Rachel isn't you."

"And he told your father what I'd shown him. It seemed as though Graham was beginning to believe that something may have happened to me, but with Rachel showing up at my father's wake, there's no more reason for him to be suspicious."

"But Kasey knows she isn't you."

I nodded. "In the meantime, a woman shows up that looks and sounds just like me. Nobody would believe Kasey, and he knows it."

He threw his hands up. "That's just great. What am I supposed to do? Just remain trapped in here while Jeremy takes over my life?"

"Not necessarily. Jeremy has to find his son and inhabit his body if he's going to remain alive, that much we know. He has no idea who that is. Even with my ability to see the other side, I can't tell. All we can hope for is that Jeremy can't find him in time, and he'll die."

"And if his spirit dies, what happens to me?"

I shrugged. "I suppose you'd go back to your body."

"But you don't know that for sure and neither do I. What's Jeremy doing now?"

I sighed. "I don't want to know."

"It might help us find out if he knows who his son is yet."

"I'm pretty sure he doesn't, but you're right. We need to know for sure."

I closed my eyes and concentrated on Jeremy. I found him in the hallway outside Irma's room, talking to the maid, Greta. They were talking about her.

"She stays in her bedroom most of the time," Greta said. "She's frail both mentally and physically. She probably won't even remember that she has a son."

Jeremy put his hand up. "Say no more, Greta. I can handle my mother."

He entered her master bedroom while Greta waited outside the door. The room appeared the same as it had been when he and his father were alive. Nothing had changed from what he could see. The room was still full of antique furniture, painted lamps and sculptures from Europe. Hung on the walls were his mother's favorite paintings, centuries old, which she had purchased during her travels to Croatia.

He walked up to the bed as the sun was setting. It was still light enough in her room for him to see her, though, and he pulled up a chair next to her bed.

"Mother?" he whispered as he sat down. "Are you awake?"

She didn't move. He couldn't tell if she was breathing or not. He reached for her frail, wrinkled hand and whispered her name a bit louder. This time she jumped forward, her eyes open wide.

The motion startled him, and he almost burst out laughing as he witnessed the deranged expression on her face. Her white, wiry hair was standing up straight. He thought she looked like a lunatic.

"Bug-a-boo?" Irma said, her cloudy eyes searching the room. "Is that you?"

He snickered, recognizing the nickname she used to call his father. She knew Harold hated it, so she did it on purpose. She continued to stare forward with crazed eyes, not even acknowledging Jeremy's existence.

"Hello…Hello?"

He squeezed her hand again. "Mother, it's me. Your son, Jeremy."

She turned her head in his direction. Her eyes widened, and she reached for his face. She touched his cheeks and then his ears, messed up his hair and squeezed his nose hard. She moaned and reached for an old pair of glasses sitting on her nightstand, which made her eyes appear twice as large. Once she saw his face, she yanked her hand back and pulled her blanket up to her neck.

"Who the hell are you, and why are you in my bedroom?"

"Mother, I know it doesn't look like me, but I'm Jeremy, your only son. I've come back to take care of you and to bring our family members back one by one. The Wickcliffs are going to live again."

She didn't respond at first, and he wondered what she was trying to remember. "My son? I don't have a son. I have a daughter named Rachel." She grimaced. "Poor thing, she is. Ugly as sin ever since the day she was born."

He cleared his throat. "Don't you remember me at all, Mother? I was the son you always wanted. You must remember me."

"Why are you calling me mother? I've never seen you before in my life. Are you cuckoo?" She squirmed in the bed. "Oh, no! Are you some kind of pervert? You can't have my body, you know." She pulled her covers closer to herself. "I'm warning you. I'll scream!"

He sat back, shook his head and stood up. "It's alright. You don't have to scream. I'll leave."

She reached over to the side of her bed and picked up a bell, which she started ringing violently. "I'll have Velma escort you out of here immediately. I can't have strangers walking into my bedroom while I'm sleeping." She exhaled deeply when she rang the bell again. Frustrated that no one was acknowledging her call, she fell back on her pillow and let out a deep sigh. "It's impossible to find good help these days."

"I'll be back to see you," Jeremy said, walking out of her room and closing the door behind him. He found Greta standing outside the door.

She could tell by his expression that his visit with Irma didn't go as he'd hoped. "I told you."

"You were right. She's totally lost her mind. The strangest thing is that she only remembers Rachel and how she despised her."

"Her memory comes and goes in pieces. It gets worse each day."

He narrowed one eye and put his hand on his chin rubbing it. "I have to do something to help her."

Greta stared at him. "There's nothing you can do for her now. Nature's taken its course."

He glared at her with a disgusted expression, causing her to stumble backward. Then he came towards her slowly and deliberately.

"We Wickcliffs defy nature. If you don't believe that, all you have to do is take a look at me. I'm here, aren't I? I'll help my mother somehow." He sighed realizing he was wasting his breath. "I'll have to deal with her later." He began to walk down the hall. "Right now I need to go see Gracey Menze. It's time for me to find my son and bring him home."

Chapter 23

For the first time, I'd witnessed Jeremy almost behave like a human being. When he was with his mother, I saw something in his eyes that I'd never before seen: compassion. It was clear that family was his downfall, and that got me thinking about Rachel. If he had a weakness, she had to have one too.

It infuriated me that Rachel was pretending to be me. Although Kasey knew the truth, he couldn't prove anything. Her appearance undid the progress I'd made with him and with my family trying to convince them that I was in danger. As I continued to think about it, I saw her in the back of her limo.

It was dusk now, and she was thinking about how brilliant the scenery looked around her. Brilliant shades of pink and purple lit up the sky as the last few rays of sun peeked out over the horizon.

As I continued to read her thoughts, I began to see her in a different light. I'd thought of her as a vile, evil creature, whose soul matched her previous outward appearance. However, as she looked into the sunset, she relished it. She'd spent her entire life locked up in the tower room of the mansion, secluded from everything and everyone. She'd never seen a sunset before. If I hadn't been so angry and horrified about what happened to me and her role in it, I would've felt sorry for her.

Gaul looked at her in the rearview mirror. "Are you alright?"

She gave him a slow nod. "I am now." She shivered and rubbed her arms with her hands. "Turn that heat up. I can't shake this chill. It feels like death."

"How did it go?"

"I recognized a lot of people from the pictures you showed me. What you told me about Shelly's life and relationships helped. It almost went off without a hitch."

Midnight's Edge, The Secrets of Sleepy Meadows

"Almost?"

"There was a guy there...Kal...no, Kasey. He's Shelly and Ethan's friend. He looked at me strangely and told me I wasn't her. I don't know how he knew or what he meant by it. I think he might know who I am."

"That's Kasey Menze. He's the son of one of the witches that tried to destroy Jeremy all those years ago. I'm sure she taught him everything she knows. He probably has powers as she does."

"Well, we can't have him ruining our plans."

"I wouldn't worry about him. Even if he's suspicious of you, nobody will ever believe him, and he wouldn't be able to prove anything if they did. You look like Shelly, and you sound like her. In time, you'll become her to everyone else in this town. The more he rambles on about it, the more people will think that he's lost his mind. I've heard through the grapevine that kind of behavior isn't out of character for him. He was a heavy drinker."

Her eyes narrowed, and she smiled deviously. "Maybe we can use that to our advantage if he ever gets in the way of our plans."

They reached the mansion, and Gaul parked the car in front. He got out, opened the door for her, gave her his hand, and helped her out. He dropped her off at the path leading to the front steps. He got back in the car and drove off to park it in the garage.

Rachel gawked at the mansion and scowled at its current state. She noticed how dilapidated it had become. There were cracks in the windows and vines had taken over and crept over everything. Stones had fallen from the steps. It wasn't as if she'd ever seen it before in its heyday, but she remembered pictures Gaul would show her in the tower room. It had seen better days. The mansion's condition didn't matter much to her, though. She was happy to be alive, which was at my expense, something she didn't care about either. All she cared about was being out of the darkness that she'd come from. A place neither she nor Jeremy ever mentioned.

She entered the mansion and walked into the parlor, finding Jeremy staring up at the painting of himself, the very same one I'd pulled Reed out of in the attic. Now that it hung in the parlor adjacent to the fireplace, any hope I had of using it as a portal to return to the mortal realm seemed to vanish.

She still hadn't adjusted to the fact that they were both alive again and in different forms. She cleared her throat and folded her arms. "Thinking about the old days, Jeremy?"

He turned to her and smiled warmly. He approached her and took her hand in his, gazing into her eyes. "You could say that. How was the funeral? I would've given anything to be there so I could see their faces. It would've given me immense pleasure to see the Hawkinses suffering, but I didn't want to answer any questions. It was suspicious enough that I was in the room with that Hawkins bastard when he died."

"I played the grieving daughter perfectly. I almost fooled myself."

"Splendid. I knew that you'd be able to convince everyone you were Shelly." He led her over to the sofa where they sat down together.

She tilted her head to the side. "Almost everyone."

Jeremy sat back. His eyes were filled with curiosity. "What do you mean?"

"There was a young man there, Kasey Menze, who acted suspicious of me. He told me he knows I'm not Shelly."

Jeremy raised a brow. "Why would he doubt it?"

"I don't think he's like the rest of them. Gaul seems to think he has powers. He knows."

Jeremy looked away and rubbed his chin. "He'd better hope people never believe him." His eyes moved back to her. "Pursuing his suspicions would be a fatal mistake."

He suddenly stopped and grabbed his arm, wincing in pain.

"What's the matter?" Rachel asked.

He rolled up his sleeve and showed her his arm. Rachel gasped at the sight of it. The skin had turned black and blue.

It took me by surprise too. It looked as though the skin was decaying. Maybe that answered Reed's question. It wasn't just Jeremy's spirit that died if he didn't find his son; potentially Reed's body could die too. Then what would happen to his spirit? How was I going to give him the news? I tried to push those thoughts out of my mind, and I turned my attention back to Rachel.

She glared at Jeremy with wide eyes. "What's happening to you?"

He pulled down his sleeve. "This body I'm in is dying. I can't remain in it for much longer I'm afraid. It was supposed to be a temporary host. I've got to step up my efforts to find my son. I need to inhabit someone of my bloodline if I'm going to continue to live."

"What can I do?"

"There isn't anything you can do. I have to find him, and I think I know who might know where he is. I was about to head out to see Gracey Menze and make her tell me. I know she knows, and if she doesn't tell me, I'll force it out of her." He stood up. "I've got to go. I can't waste any more time."

She stood up too, grabbing his arm. "Will you be alright?"

He embraced her and then touched her cheek. "Oh, my dear sister. How I've missed you, Rachel."

She broke the embrace and stepped back. "Please, don't call me that anymore." She walked towards the fireplace and glanced at the painting of him. She pointed at it and turned back to him. "Where did this come from?"

He smiled. "It was up in the attic. I hung it back up where it belongs."

She gazed at the painting again. It brought back the feelings of jealousy she had towards her brother from their past lives. She remembered how handsome he'd been and how different life had been for her in contrast. He had everything she had wanted while she had been ostracized, cast away and trapped in her tower bedroom, treated like a sick, diseased animal that no one wanted.

Although her brother had brought her back from the dead, she secretly couldn't help but feel satisfied that she was the beautiful one now while he was stuck in a body that was decaying. She kept those thoughts to herself, however, and smiled at him.

"Call me Shelly from now on. I want to live her life—the life she so desperately wanted to end."

"Why would you want to be called by her name? You're Rachel, my sister."

She balled up her fist and held it up in front of herself. "That was a woman who was ill, grotesque, and a monster."

He approached her and put his hand on her cheek. "You were never a monster to me. I not only love you the way you are now, but I loved you then, just as you were. I didn't care what anyone else said about you or what they thought. I always tried to help you, even if Mother didn't want anyone to."

She didn't know if she believed him. She didn't remember her brother paying much mind to her. Gaul was the only one that had. "Please, if you love me, abide by my wishes. I want to forget who I used to be. I've finally got a chance to be happy."

His expression hardened. "Fine. As you wish. I never could or would deny you anything."

She smiled. "I'm ready to see Mother now."

He shook his head. "I don't know if that's such a great idea. I already had a visit with her, and I can tell you she's not well."

"Was she ever? She was always sick and twisted."

"It's worse. She's senile. She didn't even remember that she had a son."

Her right brow arched. "Really? How interesting. Now I have to see her. I've always dreamed of the day where I could make her feel as pathetic and useless as she made me feel."

"If you must see her, she's in her bedroom. Top of the stairs, the eighth door on the right. You've probably never been in there, have you?"

"I never left the tower. One time I tried, but Mother had me locked in from that point forward."

She kissed her brother on the cheek and left the parlor. She walked up the grand staircase in the foyer. As she ascended, she glanced at the paintings and pictures on the wall of family members who had long since passed. Not one painting was of her.

She remembered her mother once telling her that she was too ugly to be painted or photographed. All the hurt and resentment she had for her mother came back to her, and she realized how much she wanted her mother to pay for the suffering she had inflicted on her.

I saw Rachel's memories vividly, and they made me sick. As a child, Rachel longed for Irma's affection and love. What she got was only pain. Irma treated her as though she was nothing but a burden and a curse on the family. There came a time when Irma stopped visiting her in the tower bedroom, even while she lay dying.

Once in the long hallway that headed towards Irma's bedroom,

Rachel thought about how she had once fantasized about killing her. She decided that it was time to make her mother pay for every cruel and inhumane thing she'd ever done to her.

Before she reached her mother's door, she glanced down at the other end of the hall and saw the staircase that led to the tower bedroom. Although it terrified her, she was compelled to go there. She went down the hall to the door and began to climb the worn, wooden steps slowly. When she got to the large, heavy metal door at the top, she took in a deep breath.

She opened the door cautiously and went inside to find that nothing had changed. The dark, heavy drapes were drawn as they had always been. The smell of dust and disease lingered. She wondered how long it had been since the drapes were drawn, or the small, barred window was opened. Her eyes scanned the room, and she noticed the twin bed she'd died on, her full-length mirror and her rocking chair with her old, worn rag doll sitting on it.

She couldn't believe her mother had kept everything the same. The silence in the room disturbed her, but it was soon broken by a low, guttural voice. "Look at you. It's been a long time, but I always knew you'd come back. You belong here."

She stared into the mirror and gasped in horror. What she saw was not my face, but the ghastly reflection of what she had once been, deformed and hideous. The reflection cackled, and she put her hands over her ears turning away from the mirror. "This can't be happening."

Once the laughter had stopped, she turned to the mirror again. The ashen reflection of what she had once been was still there: her hair was black and wiry; black circles surrounded her green eyes, which were sunken in below her protruding forehead; her body was emaciated, bent, crooked at every joint. She was wearing a light-green nightgown, worn, tattered and torn.

She put her hands over her face to block out the image. The monster in the mirror pointed its long crooked finger at her and cackled again.

"You're still the same monster you always were, Rachel. Look at yourself. You can't hide from what you are, and you'll never escape it."

The anger increased in her, and she clenched her fists. "Shut up. I have escaped. Nobody's going to stop me from having the life I've always wanted. Not you, not anybody!"

She saw a glass vase on the dresser with dried flowers in it, grabbed it, and threw it at the mirror. The vase shattered against the glass leaving the mirror virtually unscathed. The horrid reflection faded away, but she was left breathless and fell to the floor, burying her face in her hands.

She huddled into the corner of the room unable to move and then heard someone coming up the stairs. Gaul entered and saw her on the floor. He knelt down beside her and ran his hand over her head. She remembered his touch, the feeling of his large hands upon her and nestled into him putting her head on his shoulder.

"I'm here," he said, cradling her. "You're not alone anymore."

She wrapped her arms around him, thankful that he was there to comfort her just as he had done in private before. She remembered how well he'd cared for her and believed he had been the only one who ever truly loved her. Although her brother had just said that he had always cared for her, she didn't believe him. What she remembered was a look of pity he gave her the few times he came to her room. It wasn't the same as loving her or caring for her. Most of the time, he'd been too concerned with his desires to bother with her meager existence. She'd come to realize that Gaul was her only true friend. He was the only one who had ever accepted her as she had once been.

While Gaul held her in his arms, she finally knew how much they made sense together. They were both monsters, mistreated by her family, banished and enslaved. He was the only one she could trust. They were alike in so many ways, and they were finally together again.

I'd known that if I followed Rachel, I'd find out what her weakness was. She was afraid of what she'd been, of the life she was so desperate to leave behind. Now that I knew what it was, I had to find a way to make it work to my advantage.

Chapter 24

I'd learned earlier in the night that Gracey called Kasey and asked him to come over to her house. She was planning on telling him the truth about where he'd come from and that his presence in Sleepy Meadows could put him in danger if Jeremy knew about him. At least I knew that she'd be safe if Jeremy showed up with her son to protect her.

By the time Jeremy left his house, it was dark, and he assumed that he'd be able to sneak around Gracey's house unnoticed. He exhaled sharply and buttoned up his coat. It was a cold night, and the sky was clear. Stars lit up the night sky, and the crescent moon shone brightly, illuminating the mansion enough to see all the cracks in the foundation.

He thought that the conditions of the grounds were deplorable, and about his mother and how her health had declined. Once a powerful, rich socialite living in an elegant home admired by all, she was now a withered old woman who was living in a dilapidated, stone prison. He vowed that things wouldn't always be that way. Finding his son was going to be the first step to his family's resurgence.

Fifteen minutes later, he reached Gracey's house and parked down the street. It was even darker than before, which would, he thought, allow him to creep around incognito. He walked towards her house casually with his head bowed down, his hands in his pockets, trying to be inconspicuous.

He went around to the back of the house, and as he approached the back door, he heard Hilda's voice. Bitterness enveloped him. She'd been the most powerful of all the women who tried to destroy him, and he resented the fact that she was still alive. He swore that she wouldn't be for long. He blamed her and Gracey for turning Lucy against him. That had been the beginning of the end for him. He blamed them single-handedly for being responsible for his death and vowed he'd make them pay.

He'd expected Gracey to be alone, and he was frustrated that she wasn't. It wasn't going to be as easy to acquire the information he needed as he had thought. He thought about leaving and coming back when she was alone and vulnerable. He looked inside her kitchen window and saw the ladies talking. When he heard the back door unlock, he hid in the bushes.

Gracey and Hilda stepped outside, and he heard them talking clearly.

"It's a cold but clear night," Gracey said, rubbing her arms. "Lovely view of the stars, isn't it, Hilda?"

"It is."

"Kasey should be here any moment. I'm so nervous. I don't even know where to start with him."

"You can never go wrong with the truth. It's about time he knows who he is, don't you think?"

Gracey nodded. "I just worry about him. He's having terrible visions again. He's sensitive and fragile in many ways. What if the truth's too much for him to bear? I'm afraid that he'll fall apart, start drinking again."

"He's strong like both of his mothers. He's going to be fine."

Jeremy peered out from the bushes at the two frail women. He couldn't get over how weak they appeared. He was going to delight in watching them crumble and fall. Jeremy was confident that this time they wouldn't escape. He watched them sit down in some lawn chairs on the back patio and continued to listen.

"Have you thought about what you're going to say?" Hilda said.

"I'm not going to mince words," Gracey said. "I'm just going to tell him that Lucy was his mother. He needs to know what she sacrificed to save his life."

Jeremy put his hand over his mouth to stifle his surprise. It was no wonder why Kasey knew that Rachel wasn't me. Kasey was special; he was a Wickcliff.

I couldn't believe what I'd heard either. Kasey was one of the most compassionate men I'd ever known. We'd been raised as family, and if this were true, he had the blood of one of the evilest, vile men I'd ever known coursing through his veins. He took after his mother Gracey because she raised him, so the Wickcliffs didn't influence him. But now that Jeremy knew about him, how long would it be before that would change?

Jeremy almost burst out from behind the bushes at this revelation, his rage increasing with every word they spoke. Instead, he took in a deep breath and kept control of himself.

Hilda took Gracey's hand in hers. "You gave up a lot too. You took Kasey into your home. You raised him as your own."

Gracey smiled. "Not only would I have done anything for Lucy, but Kasey's just as much my son in my heart as he would be if I'd have given birth to him myself. I got a good deal."

"If Jeremy finds out, he'll come looking for him. We have to protect him."

Jeremy realized now that the witches were aware of his presence, but they still didn't know what form he'd taken. He was still safe.

"I'm chilled," Gracey said, rubbing her arms. "My old bones can't handle this cold air."

"Here, take my shawl." Hilda wrapped her shawl around Gracey's shoulders. Their eyes met, and they were silent for a moment. "Let's go inside. The last thing we need is for you to get sick. We all need to be in tip-top condition if we're going to defeat Jeremy."

Once Jeremy heard the back door shut and saw that they were inside, he came out from behind the bushes, delighted that he'd learned who his son was, but also furious about all the time he had lost with him because of Lucy and the witches.

He groaned when his arm began to throb. He looked down at it and noticed that the veins were protruding. His skin was turning gray. Reed's body was dying, and he knew he was running out of time.

He looked around the yard, needing to get out of there. Now that he'd heard that Kasey was his son, he had to go somewhere private to formulate his plan to take over his body and his life. He walked backward towards the gate, not taking his eyes off the two women whom he could still see through the kitchen window. All he could think about was making them suffer.

As he whipped around to exit the gate, he saw a young man standing there. He was startled and jumped back.

Kasey grabbed his arm. "I'm sorry I scared you, Reed. What are you doing here?"

"I...um..."

"What is it?"

Jeremy wiped the sweat from his forehead, even though it was a chilly night, he was sweating profusely. "I don't feel well."

"Obviously not. You're looking at me like you've never seen me before."

Jeremy rubbed his temple. "You startled me that's all."

"Did you come to see my mother?"

"Gracey?"

Kasey shrugged. "Who else?"

"Kasey?"

Kasey looked at him strangely. "Yeah?"

"This was a mistake. I should go." He pushed past Kasey, went through the gate, and ran away. He didn't look back, but could hear Kasey yell after him.

Jeremy made it around the block to the car. He got in and sped off. As he drove back to the mansion, he thought about how young, strong and handsome Kasey appeared. Now he knew who his son was, where he was, and what he looked like. He was the perfect one to carry on the Wickcliff legacy. As he drove, he thought that it would be perfect to use Kasey's relationship with Reed to trap him. He'd get him alone and then take the steps necessary to transfer his life force into him.

A few minutes later, Jeremy pulled into the driveway of the mansion. He turned off the car and clutched the steering wheel. He was confident that everything was falling into place which had me scared for Kasey.

Although it was difficult for me to believe that someone like Kasey could be Jeremy's son, it had to be true. I had to find a way to warn him of the danger he was in.

Coming in November, 2015 from Melange Books, LLC

The 2nd book of Midnight's Edge, The Possession

Midnight's Edge, The Secrets of Sleepy Meadows

About the Authors:

David Chappuis was born in Waterloo, Iowa and grew up on a farm in Madrid, New York. He received a bachelor's degree in English/Writing and Art/Studio from Potsdam College. He has made a living as a professional web designer and resides in southern Virginia.

Michael Klinger was born in Niagara Falls, New York. He received an associate's degree in human services from Niagara County Community College and a bachelor's degree in human services management from the University of Phoenix. He currently resides in southern Virginia.

Authors Contacts:

Author Website: www.davidchappuis.com
Midnight's Edge Site: www.midnightsedgeweb.com
Twitter: www.twitter.com/davechappuis
Pinterest: https://www.pinterest.com/davechappuis/
Facebook: https://www.facebook.com/midnightsedge

CPSIA information can be obtained at www.ICGtesting.com
Printed in the USA
BVOW08s2018210716

456404BV00001BA/16/P

9 781680 461572